A MORGAN FOR MELINDA

A Morgan
for
Melinda

a novel by
DORIS GATES

The Viking Press
New York

First published in 1980 by The Viking Press
625 Madison Avenue, New York, N.Y. 10022
Published simultaneously in Canada by
Penguin Books Canada Limited
Printed in U.S.A.
3 4 5 84 83 82 81

Library of Congress Cataloging in Publication Data
Gates, Doris. A Morgan for Melinda.
Summary: Even though ten-year-old Melinda fears
riding, her father buys her a horse, and it is only
through her friendship with an elderly writer that
Melinda overcomes her fear.
[1. Horses—Fiction. 2. Friendship—Fiction.
3. Old age—Fiction] I. Title.
PZ7.G216Mo 1980   [Fic]   79–19786   ISBN 0–670–48932–8

This book is dedicated to the horses

Choco
Little Vic
Aranaway Ethan
Oakhill's Merry Jo

and the horse people
who gave me the happiest years of my life.

D. G.

Contents

A MORGAN FOR MELINDA

I

My First Ride

This book is about me, Melinda Ross, my father, and a horse. Of course my mother is in it, too, and Missy. Especially Missy. If it weren't for her I wouldn't be writing this book at all. When I told Missy I couldn't decide whether to be an airline stewardess or a writer when I grew up, she gave me good advice.

"You'll have to wait a good many years to become an airline stewardess. But you can start writing right now," she said.

Missy, being a writer, knows all there is to know about writing.

"Read and write," she told me. "Write anything—letters, keep a diary, start a book."

So I am starting this book about what happened to me beginning last year when I was ten and which is going right on happening.

But first you have to know about my father.

He's a rural mail carrier and a very nice man. His name is Calvin Ross, and he is absolutely nuts about horses. I'm not, and that's my problem. My father goes to work at five-thirty every morning except Saturday and Sunday. He comes home every afternoon around three-thirty. He waited a long time for the chance to be a rural mail carrier and worked as best he could until he got the job. And the reason he wanted that particular job was because it gave him time every day for a horse. But at no time did he ever say he wanted the horse for himself. He wanted it for me. That's my problem. You see, I don't like horses. I'm afraid of them. Did you ever stand alongside a horse? They're big. And powerful. An average-size horse weighs over a thousand pounds. And it's all muscle. They also have big teeth and feet.

When my father first announced he was buying me a horse, I said, "Thanks a lot. The last thing I want is a horse."

"Of course you want a horse," he came right back at me. "All girls want a horse. You couldn't be my daughter and not want one."

"Why can't you just get one for yourself and forget about me?" I asked.

"Because I want the fun of teaching you to ride and to care for a horse. You're built to ride. I'll take great pride in having a daughter who is a good horsewoman."

I suppose I could have gone crying to my mother and been difficult about the whole thing. The trouble is I love my father and want him to be proud of me. But there's another reason why I didn't go crying to my mother.

Five years ago I had a brother, Martin, who was five years older than I. Five years ago he died of leukemia. I can barely remember him. But I can remember that even when he was terribly ill and in bed all the time, he used to talk with my father about when he would be well and Dad would have the post office job and he could have a horse. It makes my throat sort of ache now when I think about it.

Well, of course he never got the horse. But three years after he was gone, my father got the job carrying mail on Route Two and right away started talking about getting me a horse. And because of Martin I didn't feel like fighting him about it.

A few months ago my mother went to work in an architect's office in Carmel to help pay for this house my father bought recently up the Carmel Valley. It's at the very end of the long, steep, winding road leading into a subdivision called Toro Estates. Once the whole area was a small cattle ranch, and our house is the old ranch house. Beyond it are open fields and hills and trails leading over the hills clear to Salinas. Even though the house was old and needed a lot of things done to it, my mother wasn't against buying it. We got it at a good price considering that an old barn and three acres went with it.

One Saturday when we had finally gotten settled into the old house, my father said to me, "Melinda, I've decided to introduce you to a horse today."

My heart turned over in my chest. "Where?" I asked.

"For starters we'll stop off at the red barn. You know, that place on the right-hand side of the valley road about two miles from Highway One. There are pastures on both sides of the barn with horses in them. I presume that one pasture is for mares and one for geldings."

Once upon a time, long ago when he was young, my father ran a riding academy. He knows all there is to know about horses and riding.

"I haven't done my work yet," I said, glad for once Mom has certain duties for me to perform every Saturday. One of these is changing the beds. It's nothing to change my bed, but Dad and Mom have a king-size, and I'll bet I walk a full mile around that thing getting the clean sheets and covers back on. But this particular morning I actually looked forward to that job.

"Melinda," Mom called out from the kitchen, "if your dad wants you to go with him now, I'll change the beds. Run along, dear."

"And leave you with all this work?" I demanded. "The horse can wait." And the longer the better, I thought. Maybe if I made the jobs last long enough, Dad would forget about the red barn and its horses.

No such luck. An hour later he came in from the old barn looking as happy as a hippie's dog. I had started dusting the living room furniture. This is another one of my Saturday jobs. Dad does the vacuuming.

"Melinda, that old barn is going to work out just great. There are three stalls. We'll fix one for your horse and use one for tack."

"Tack?" I said, looking around from the TV set.

"Yes. Saddles, bridles, halters, blankets."

"Great," I said, going back to my dusting.

"How much longer are you going to be?"

I started to think of all the things I might still be working at, but Mom came into the room and spoiled everything.

"Out," she said. "Vamoose, both of you. I have things to do."

So out we went. We got into Mom's VW and started down the steep Estates road.

Just before we came to the valley road, we passed Diana Morton's place. She's my best friend. I don't like her very well, but I'm in love with her brother, Dwight. Of course, he doesn't know I'm alive, because he is sixteen now and reserve pitcher on the high school varsity. When Dad first brought up the horse thing, I thought this might be a way of making Dwight take some notice of me. If he loved horses (and some boys do), and I had one and he didn't, then if I let him ride mine it could cement a beautiful relationship between us. But when I asked

Dwight, he said, "No!" very quickly and firmly and didn't even bother to look at me.

Yes, Dwight was there running the lawn mower. I leaned over quick and honked the horn, and he looked up but didn't wave. I guess he needed both hands on the mower.

As we rounded a turn of the valley road and the red barn came into view, I had a sinking feeling. I can't describe it, but I felt as if the bottom had dropped out of everything. I was going to have to pat a horse and not act like a fool in order to save my father's pride. But I loved my father and I wasn't about to let him down, fear or no fear.

A gray-haired man with blue eyes, wearing very clean blue jeans and a starched blue shirt and a white straw cowboy hat, greeted us. He was also wearing dusty cowboy boots with spurs.

Dad introduced us, and the man, who gave his name as Dodge Rayburn, shook hands. I know my hand was limp as a dead fish in his, and I felt awfully foolish.

"I've decided to buy Melinda a horse and I thought we might start looking here," Dad said for openers.

The man crossed his arms, looked off toward the

valley road, and said as if to no one in particular, "We got a few."

"What do you have to pay for a horse these days?" Dad asked.

We were standing right in front of the red barn and Dodge Rayburn leaned a shoulder against the edge of the barn door and looked sharply at Dad.

"Depends on what you want," he said.

"We want a nice horse. A nice horse doesn't cost any more to keep than a scrub."

"That's right. Any idea in mind about what you want to pay?"

Dad thought a minute. "I have decided that seven hundred and fifty dollars is my top price. Could I buy anything decent for that?"

The man unfolded his arms and moved away from the barn door. "You should be able to get a pretty nice grade horse for that. You want a registered horse, you gotta pay more."

We were moving now across the barnyard to the riding ring where, beyond it, a lot of horses were grazing. In another corral alongside the riding ring were three horses, each a bright coppery color.

"Those are nice-looking geldings," Dad said.

Dodge Rayburn smiled. "Yeah. They're three-year-old quarter horses. Each of 'em worth around thirty-five hundred dollars."

Dad whistled softly. "Out of our class, I'm afraid."

At the gate of the riding ring Mr. Rayburn picked a rope halter off the post.

"I got a palomino in the pasture beyond might do for you."

He led us down the length of the sandy ring to the far gate leading into the pasture. At the sight of him, about a dozen horses started trotting toward us. He opened the gate and, moving quietly, approached a huge horse about the color of molasses candy with a creamy mane and tail. He looked as if he had a lot of miles on him. His lower lip hung loose and his back had a dip in it. I glanced over at Dad and saw a dubious look on his face. This was not my idea of a nice horse, and I didn't think it was his, either.

Mr. Rayburn slipped the halter over the horse's head and led him toward us.

"This is Sam," he said, introducing us. "He's twelve years old and very reliable. Good trail horse. No bad habits. I've had him around for six months now. Course, he's been out in pasture and ain't cleaned up proper. But he's sound." He looked

11

around at me. "Like to try him out?"

"Maybe some other . . ." I started to say, but Dad interrupted me.

"A good idea. If it's not too much trouble, Mr. Rayburn, could you slap a saddle on him and let Melinda walk him around a bit?"

"Sure thing. He goes English or Western."

"English, please," said Dad.

My mouth was so dry I couldn't even get a word out or I would have begged like fury to be let off. I wanted to turn tail and run out of that ring so fast you could only have seen the dust of my passing. But I wouldn't let Dad down. I even moved over toward Sam and laid a hand on what I know now was his withers. Since it was early March, he hadn't lost all his winter coat. But his hide felt warm and friendly.

We all trooped back to the barn, Mr. Rayburn walking quickly, Sam following along like the reliable horse he was said to be. Mr. Rayburn brushed him off a little, then saddled and bridled him. He turned to me.

"Ever done any ridin'?"

I shook my head.

"Better use the mountin' block then."

He led Sam past the barn to where a large tree stump stood off by itself. He maneuvered the horse alongside it and held out a hand to me. I stepped up onto the stump.

"Take the reins in your left hand and grab hold of some mane," he told me. I did. "Now put your left foot in the stirrup and swing yourself up."

I did. He had hold of Sam, so I didn't have to worry about the horse walking off with me before I was ready. Suddenly there I was, feeling as if I were astraddle the ridgepole of the barn. The saddle was almost flat. Not a thing to hang onto.

"Put your foot in the other stirrup," commanded Mr. Rayburn.

I fumbled around and finally got my foot into the right stirrup. Mr. Rayburn stepped back. Sam stood like a rock. I glanced around at Dad and he was grinning all over himself. Mr. Rayburn showed me how to arrange the reins between the little finger and third finger of each hand.

"Now shorten your reins and press your knees into him gently," he said. I did and Sam started forward.

The moment I felt him moving under me, I began to panic. I knew I was going to fall off. It felt like sitting in a chair you knew was going to tip over any second. All I had to hang onto were the reins and I hung onto them for dear life. I didn't realize that I was pulling, but of course I was and poor Sam was completely confused. I had given him the signal to go forward, and now I was pulling on the reins. Obviously, that meant to back. And he began to back.

"Let up on your reins!" I heard Mr. Rayburn yell. "You'll pull him over."

At that instant Dad was at Sam's head. "Drop your reins," he commanded. I dropped them as if they were hot potatoes. "Now pick them up and hold them loosely." I picked them up. He took hold of one rein near Sam's bit and began leading him forward.

If I couldn't hang onto the reins, I had to hang onto something. There was a little rise in the saddle where it fitted over Sam's withers. I slipped my hands into this space and sort of steadied myself. Now Sam was walking steadily, and I began to get the rhythm of his walk. It was the weirdest sensation I have ever known. You could feel each step he took, but it wasn't bumpy. Not exactly. And without my even trying to, my body began moving backward and forward in rhythm with the horse's steps. We walked down toward the mares' pasture on the opposite side of the barn from where Sam had come.

Dad stopped Sam at last and turned to look up at me.

"How are you doing?"

I shook my head. My mouth was too dry for words.

Dad took his hand off the rein. "Now pull easy on your left rein and turn him around."

Gathering up all my courage, I did as he said. In fact, I pulled so easy that Sam didn't feel it. I pulled a little harder and good old Sam turned himself carefully around and slowly walked back to the barn. Dad walked along beside me. "You're lookin' good," said Mr. Rayburn as we came up to where he waited.

The only thing that could have made Dad look happier was having Martin restored to him. It was clear to me that he considered the battle won and that now I was really on my way to becoming a horsewoman. Only he couldn't see inside me. I was scared. I was so scared that I couldn't even say I wanted to get off. My mouth was still so dry my tongue couldn't form words.

"Like to walk down to the ring and trot him

around a little?" asked Mr. Rayburn.

Trot him around! Suddenly I found my voice. "How do I get off?" I asked.

"Hey, wait a minute, Melinda," said Dad, coming toward me. "You haven't been on long enough to get the feel of him. Let's go into the ring for a few minutes so you can get the feel of him and begin to relax."

"He's a nice, quiet horse," Mr. Rayburn assured me. "You got nothin' to worry about."

Well, the long and the short of it was that we walked back to the ring. Mr. Rayburn was taking a phone call inside the barn, so Dad walked at Sam's head. He looked back at me and grinned.

"You look really great, Melinda. You have a natural seat."

What was he talking about? Of course I had a natural seat. I was born with it. It was my own personal bottom and the right size for a girl of ten who was tall for her age.

We went inside the ring and Dad shut the gate. I sat all alone on Sam trying to remember not to pull on the reins.

"In the ring you always ride close to the rail," Dad said as he rejoined us. "Now get him over to the rail and keep him there."

The ring was oblong, and we were in the middle of it just inside the gate. I didn't know whether he wanted me to go to the left or to the right. And besides, I didn't know how to get there.

"Which side?" I asked.

"Turn him to the right."

I pulled gently on the right rein and after thinking it over for a moment, Sam went slowly over to the right side of the ring, Dad still walking beside me.

From the moment I had got on him, I had hardly taken my eyes off Sam's ears. Somewhere I had heard that you can tell what a horse is thinking about by watching his ears. Sam's flopped comfortably out at the sides. Sometimes he turned one toward me, but he never pricked them forward or laid them back.

Dad chuckled once. "I think Sam would like you to say something to him. I just now saw him turn an ear toward you. Go on—talk to him."

What did you say to a horse? How could you say it when your mouth was so dry your tongue stuck to its roof?

I ran my dry tongue along my dry lips. "Hi, Sam," I managed to croak.

If Sam heard me, he paid no attention but went faithfully plodding on.

We went along all three sides of the ring and were back at the gate again.

"Now I'm going to stand in the middle of the ring," Dad said, "and watch you ride Sam by yourself. Just give him his head and try to get the feel of him as he walks along. He knows what to do."

After going twice around the ring by myself, I worked up enough courage to lift my eyes from Sam's ears. I looked around me. Wooded hills rose up sharply from the north side of the barnyard. I could see traffic moving on the valley road opposite the hills. I finished the third circling of the ring and pulled up beside Dad.

"How do I get off?" I asked for the second time. They were almost the only words I had spoken since we arrived at the barn.

In answer, Dad started for the gate and Sam followed him without a signal from me. He went through it and across the barnyard and straight to the bar where he had been saddled, and stopped with a thankful sigh.

Dad went to his head. "Keep your reins," he said, "and take your right foot out of the stirrup. Then, standing in your left stirrup, swing your right foot over Sam's rump. Lean into the saddle and take your left foot out of its stirrup and slide to the ground."

I managed to do all this, but sliding down the side of Sam was like going belly down on a toboggan, and I landed with a thump that hurt my feet.

Mr. Rayburn appeared and took off Sam's bridle while Dad unbuckled the saddle girth. While the two men were putting away the tack in a big room off the stall part of the barn, I stood looking at Sam. I tried to sort out my feelings about him. I knew I didn't actually dislike him. I knew he had been very good and kind to me. He hadn't taken one wrong step. If ever I could bring myself to like a horse, I thought I would like Sam. If I had to have a horse (and it appeared that I did), then maybe Sam was the horse I should have. I felt sure I could trust him. Standing there with one hind foot sort of tucked under him and his lower lip hanging loose, he didn't look as if he would ever jump or shy at anything.

"Well, what do you think of him?" said Mr. Rayburn, coming up behind me. He was smiling and his eyes were kind.

"I sort of like him," I replied.

"He's a good horse. You can canter him for an

hour at a time and he won't ever change speed. And he won't stop either. He'll just keep goin' steady as a clock. Just the kind of horse you want when you're startin' out to ride."

"Yes, he is a good horse," said Dad. "What are you asking for him?"

"Four hundred dollars."

"A fair price," said Dad. "But I think we'd like to look around a little bit. He's the first horse we've seen."

"Sure. It pays to look around," said Mr. Rayburn.

Dad thanked him for his kindness. We each patted Sam and then we drove away.

As we started down the long, straight, potholed drive to the valley road, Dad said, speaking slowly, "Now let me see. There's a stable somewhere on Aguajito road. They might have some horses for sale there."

I spoke up quickly. "Dad, please, can't we just skip it for today? I think I've had all the horse I want for one day."

We had reached the end of the drive and he stopped to check the traffic. We had to wait almost a minute before we could go forward.

"Are you that shook up over your first ride?"

"Yes, I am. I could maybe go back and ride Sam again. But I don't feel up to another strange horse right now. You've just got to understand, Dad."

He nodded and made a left turn, heading home. "It's just hard for me to understand people who are afraid of horses, that's all. Especially my own kid." He looked sort of grim as he said that last, and I knew he was thinking about Martin.

"Maybe we ought to settle for Sam," I said quickly, to take his mind off his sorrow. "He's lots less than you planned to pay and I do sort of like him. I think he understands me."

Dad laughed. "I'm sure he does, Melinda. A wise old horse like Sam has seen a lot of riders come and go. He's learned to size them up and to take care of himself."

"Then why don't we just buy him?"

Dad thought for a minute. He looked a little uncomfortable.

"To tell you the truth, Melinda, I would like a horse for you with a little more spirit than Sam. I believe you're a natural rider. I never saw a girl look so good in the saddle her first time out. I want to school you in equitation. And Sam can hardly be

21

considered an equitation mount. And I think he's a little big for you. He's at least sixteen hands and heavy-boned. I'd like something a bit more elegant."

"In other words," I said, "you'd like one that would be a little more fun for *you* to ride."

"Well, yes, if you want to put it that way. And once you'd learned how to ride, you'd find Sam rather dull. A horse with some spirit doesn't need to be any less dependable than Sam."

"It's going to be a long time before I'm ready for a horse with spirit," I informed him as we turned into our Estates road.

I asked him to let me off when we came to Diana's place. The morning was shot. I knew Dwight would be gone. He had a game that afternoon. But Diana and I might have time for a swim before lunch. She has a swimming pool and lets me keep my bikini in their poolside cabana. She's an "in," and I'm an "out."

2

Not Just a Horse

I suppose that 1976 will go down in the history books as the Bicentennial Year, when our country celebrated its two hundredth birthday. But for me it will always be the Year of the Horse. And of Missy. But Missy doesn't come into this book yet.

At Valley Hills School where I was in the fifth grade, we had been celebrating the Bicentennial just about ever since school started up again after Christmas. Every week there was something going on to remind us that the United States had weathered wars and riots and droughts and floods and good harvests and bad harvests and just about anything else you could think of and had survived.

Well, the very Monday following my first ride, they showed a film at our school in celebration of the Bicentennial. The film was called *Justin Morgan Had a Horse*, and it was based on a book, I learned later, with the same title. It all took place way back in our country's history and was about a Morgan horse. His owner was a man named Justin Morgan.

I followed the other kids into the multipurpose room, dragging my feet. The last thing I wanted to see on that particular Monday was a film about a horse. But the more I watched, the more I began to enjoy the thing. There was a little foal in the film that was just about the darlingest animal I had ever seen, even if it was a baby horse. And later, when it grew up to be a full-grown horse, it still was small. That is, it was small compared to Sam. I began to think, about the time the film ended, that if I could have a Morgan horse, I wouldn't be so dead set against having a horse at all.

That evening at dinner I told my parents about the film. I didn't tell them the whole story because there's nothing in this world so boring as to have to listen to someone telling you about a movie or a TV show he's seen. But I did make the point that if I could have a Morgan, I wouldn't object so much to having a horse or trying to ride.

"We couldn't afford to buy a Morgan," Dad said.

"Do you know about Morgans?" I asked him.

"Yes, I do. There isn't any horse I'd rather have if I could afford it than a Morgan. They're great horses; they can do anything. And they are beautiful."

"Then why not look for one?" my mother asked.

"Because, my dear Lynn, you couldn't possibly buy a Morgan for less than a thousand dollars, and it would probably be twice that much."

"But you won't really know unless you've inquired," she persisted. "Are there any Morgan stables anywhere near us?"

"The closest one's about thirty miles from here. Morgan Manor. Their top stallion is Waseeka Peter Piper."

Mom smiled down the table at him. "How come you know so much?"

He smiled back at her as he took a sip of wine. (My parents always have wine with dinner, but that's about all they ever drink. Except, of course, tea and coffee.)

"You wouldn't expect an old horseman to pass up a horse show. Now would you?"

She shook her head at him, still smiling teasingly.

"The Morgan horse people have a show in Monterey every July, and I've attended three of them. Morgan Manor always brings a lot of horses. And wins a lot of ribbons."

"How about visiting Morgan Manor sometime?" suggested Mom.

"Would you like to, Lynn?" Dad asked, setting down his wine glass and looking suddenly very enthusiastic.

"Of course I would. How about next Sunday?"

"Done and done," he cried. And he rushed right away from the table and into the kitchen. In a minute or two we heard him putting in a call to the Towerses, who, apparently, he knew to be the owners of Morgan Manor.

Mom and I didn't make any bones about listening in on the conversation, and by the time he returned to the table we knew that the coming Sunday would see us at Morgan Manor. Even though he couldn't afford to own one, Dad could be almost perfectly happy devoting a Sunday to Morgan horses.

As the days passed (and they went quickly because I wasn't looking forward to our visit to Morgan Manor), I began to realize that my interest in having a Morgan was more a delaying action than anything else. I did think that little foal in the movie was cute and all that. But I think in my bones I knew that if I began to want not just a horse but a special kind of horse, it would take longer to find it. My scheme as Sunday drew near was to fall in love with one of the Morgan Manor horses and then plead with my Dad to save up until we could afford to own it. Or one very like it.

Sunday morning Mom got up early and fried chicken. She always sees that there are plenty of drumsticks for Dad and me. She made a salad, put in some breadsticks and fruit, and there was our picnic lunch.

But first there was church.

We go to church in the Carmel Valley village. Our priest is Father John, and we love him because he loves everybody. Church is fairly boring, but when Father John extends his hands toward us and says, "May the peace of the Lord be with you *always*," you feel as if maybe it will. Kneeling that Sunday with my mother on one side of me and my father on the other, I felt, as I always feel when we are together in church, unusually safe and cared for. We're all so busy during the week that we don't see much of one another except at dinnertime. But every Sunday morning we are a really and truly "together" family. And I like it. I looked at each of them and I thought I could tell that they were praying for Martin and probably for me. I prayed for all three of them and then I prayed that I might get over my fear of horses and be a credit to my father.

It took less than an hour to reach Morgan Manor. The first thing we saw when we turned off 101 onto the Towerses' county road was their huge barn lying up against the side of a hill. As we approached, the hill moved farther back and the barn got bigger. Three dogs of no special breed came out to greet us. They were barking noisily, but their tails were wagging. Dad got out of the car just as a youngish woman, who turned out to be Mrs. Towers, came out of the barn. Close up, I decided she was about the age of my mother, who is thirty-five. She was very pretty, with blond hair cut short and gray-blue eyes set wide apart. She smiled at Dad, and they shook hands. Mom and I got out of the car and she greeted us.

"So you think you want a Morgan, Melinda?"

I itched to say, "No, I don't. I don't want any horse at all." But what I did was smile back at her and nod my head. What a hypocrite!

"I think I'd better make our position clear before we waste any of your time," said Dad. "We want to get a nice horse for Melinda. But we only have seven hundred and fifty dollars to put into it." He smiled his special boyish smile that always made him look ten years younger. "Would you have a Morgan at that price?"

"Definitely," declared Mrs. Towers, and my heart sank.

So much for the delaying action! So much for saving up to get just the horse I wanted! All shot, and we hadn't been here ten minutes!

"Come on into the barn," she directed, leading the way, and we went three abreast behind her. Dad was looking jubilant. Mom just looked interested. I'm sure by the feel of my face that it was saying plainly, "Yuck!"

The barn was as big on the inside as it looked on the outside. You could have parked a dozen school buses in it and had lots of room left over. Down both sides were stalls, and over each half door was a horse's head, each turned our way. Light came from the two wide doors at each end and from windows set high up near the roof. It smelled of dust and hay and horse. Not unpleasant, actually. The floor, if you could call it that, seemed to be a mixture of sand and sawdust. Just right, I supposed, for horses' feet.

Mrs. Towers led us across the barn to a stall halfway down its length. She gently pushed aside the head of the horse reaching for her over the half door and looked down in the stall.

"This is Mantic Peter Frost," she said. "I'll sell him as a weanling for seven hundred and fifty dollars."

We came up to the stall and looked inside. I confess I caught my breath in pure surprise. There, pressed close to his mother's side, was a little foal even cuter than the one in the movie. He had a dainty small head and a tiny soft muzzle which he lifted to me. I put my hand on it and felt his breath. His little ears were pricked forward, and his big brown eyes were completely unafraid. He seemed as friendly as a kitten.

I turned to my father. "Oh, Dad, let's buy him."

At that moment all I knew was that I wanted that little foal. I just wanted to have him around to look at. And to pet and to play with.

"He's sure cute," Dad said, "but it would be a long time before you could ride him."

As if that were a drawback! All at once I could see real purpose in my wanting him. If I had to wait for Mantic Peter Frost to grow up, it would be some time before I would be required to ride him.

"You couldn't ride him at all for two years," Dad explained.

"I don't care," I declared, and never felt more sincere. "I just want to raise him and get to know him, and by the time he is ready to ride, I won't have any fear of him at all."

"Are you a beginning rider?" asked Mrs. Towers. I nodded.

"We have some older stock that might be just right for you," she said, "but I'm afraid not at your price."

Then Mom spoke. "It seems to me, Cal, that if you want Melinda to learn about horse care and become familiar with horses, you could do worse than to buy this little fellow." I have never wanted to hug my mother as much as I did then.

Dad sort of glared at her.

"But it would be completely impractical, Lynn. She should be riding right now if she's ever going to develop into a true horsewoman. Every year we postpone it will make it harder for her."

Mom smiled, a slow, understanding smile. "Why don't you admit it, Cal? You're buying a horse once for Melinda and twice for yourself."

Dad returned that smile a little sheepishly and shrugged. "Okay. I do want to get her a horse we can both enjoy. But it's not fair to say it's once for her and twice for me."

"We won't belabor the point," said Mom, looking knowingly at Mrs. Towers, who returned much the same kind of look. Poor Dad. Up against three women.

"If you really want a Morgan," began Mrs. Towers, "I can put you on to one cheap."

"Tell me more," said Dad.

"Are you familiar with a certain cattle ranch away up the Carmel Valley called the Granite Ranch?" she asked Dad.

"I ought to be," he returned. "It's on my mail route."

"Okay. They own a seven-year-old registered Morgan stallion that they want to sell for three hundred dollars."

"What's wrong with it?" asked Dad.

"Not a thing," returned Mrs. Towers. "Only it's never been ridden. They thought we might be interested in him, especially at the price, but he's outside our line of breeding."

"Have you ever seen him?" asked Dad.

She shook her head. "I've been told that he's a chestnut, around fifteen hands, and a very good-looking, typey Morgan."

Dad glanced at Mom, but he wasn't really seeing her. He looked as if he were trying to believe the best news he had ever heard. "A registered Morgan for three hundred dollars! It's unbelievable!" There was awe in his voice. He turned back to Mrs. Towers. "Why are they getting rid of him?"

"That's a fair question. It seems they introduced him into their herd of brood mares four years ago. Now they have all the young stuff they want and no longer need him."

"Could I call them from your phone? I want that stallion before anyone else gets him."

"Cal, are you crazy?" Mom spoke sharply. "You can't be thinking of letting Melinda learn to ride on a seven-year-old unbroken stallion!"

"Don't worry, Lynn. By the time he's ready for Melinda, he will be broken and gentle and he won't be a stallion."

As Mom and I followed Dad and Mrs. Towers

toward the house, I had a lovely feeling inside me. It was true I wouldn't have the foal, which I honestly would have liked to have. But it would be some time yet before I would be riding a horse.

3

The Stallion

Dad was sitting in the car waiting for me next day when the school bus pulled up to the Toro Estates stop. Diana and I got off along with some other kids. He's usually there waiting, and Diana rides as far as her house with us. Sometimes when her mother isn't home, she goes home with us and stays until her mother phones her. Today when Diana and I walked up to the car, Dad said, "I'm sorry, Diana, but I'm not going your way today. Melinda and I have a date with a horse."

"She'd rather have a date with Dwight."

Diana's full of cracks like that. Still, it gave me a

secret sort of satisfaction to have Dwight even referred to in connection with me.

"We're off to see a wild stallion," Dad said as I got into the car and Diana turned away to start the pull up to her house.

"Melinda Ross, cowgirl," she said over her shoulder and threw a pitying smile at me. I had told her all about having to have a horse when we had our swim on Saturday. She had been mildly sympathetic but not really interested. So today at school I hadn't bothered to mention the Morgan stallion. When it comes right down to it, Diana isn't interested in anything that doesn't concern her directly. If it weren't for Dwight, she wouldn't be my best friend.

"Now just what did that mean?" Dad asked, referring to the cowgirl crack.

I shrugged. "Who knows? Sometimes Diana talks just to hear her brains rattle."

I saw Dad smile, and I looked off toward the river and the hills. It's a pretty drive up the Carmel Valley. And once we had left the village and started the climb up into the hills, they were so close they seemed to be moving beside us. It reminded me of a poem we had read for creative writing. It was written by a little girl. Miss Anderson had dug up everything she could find that had been written by kids. To encourage us, I guess. Anyway, this poem by a little girl had one line I remember: "The hills are going somewhere." I had thought at the time I read it that it was a dumb way to describe hills. But now I could see she had been right. The hills *were* going somewhere. They were going right along with us.

I mentioned this to Dad and he just said, "Uh-huh," and I knew he was thinking of the stallion. Well, if Dwight had asked me to go to a movie with him next Saturday, I wouldn't want anyone talking poetry to me, either. I would just want to sit and dream about that date. And now Dad was dreaming of the stallion we were on our way to find. And to buy.

The Granite Ranch was like no cattle ranch I could even imagine. We drove into a huge yard. Off to one side under some spreading live oaks was a beautiful house. Big and rambling. There was a garden around it. Back of the house was a large pond with white swans sailing on it. You couldn't see any motion except a smooth going forward, as if some wind was blowing them along.

There was no one around. But suddenly we heard a roar and out from the shed, way off to one side, a jeep came backing toward us. It swung around in the big yard and came to a stop.

A man got out and called, "Your name Ross?"

"Right," said Dad, and went forward to shake hands.

"Chuck Railey," said the man. "I'm the foreman here."

"And this is my daughter, Melinda," said Dad.

Mr. Railey gave me a nod. "All set to go to find that stallion?" he asked.

"I guess so," I replied, feeling dumb.

"Let's go then."

Dad sat on a little jump seat behind the foreman and me.

Mr. Railey was not a large man, but he was sturdy and strong-looking. I thought he would be very good in an emergency, and this was reassuring because I had never ridden in a jeep before. It was a brand-new sensation. The sides of a jeep—this jeep, anyway—are open. It reminded me of that flat saddle Sam had worn. There was nothing to hang onto.

We drove out of the ranch yard, crossed the highway, and pulled up in front of a pasture gate.

Dad jumped out to open it, and Mr. Railey flung the jeep through. That's the only word to describe the way he drove. He seemed to think that little car would stop dead in its tracks if he didn't gun it. Dad got back in, and we started driving across the wide pasture. It seemed to go on forever, bordered on the west by the hills. Cattle were grazing in it, and they lifted their heads to look at us. There is no way you can look dumber than a cow. I had never really had a chance to study a cow before. But now I sat about on a level with their eyes as we drove past them, and stupider faces I have never seen.

I hadn't spoken a word yet, and I thought it was about time I let Mr. Railey know I wasn't completely tongue-tied. So I turned around to Dad and remarked, "Cows sure look stupid, don't they?"

"These aren't cows, honey," he replied. "They're steers."

"What's the difference between cows and steers?" I wanted to know.

Mr. Railey spoke. "You might better ask what's the difference between steers and bulls."

"Okay," I said, "what's the difference?"

"Maybe you better explain," said Mr. Railey over his shoulder to Dad.

"You can't learn any younger, Melinda," said

Dad. "And it's really very simple. Every male animal possesses organs of reproduction."

"So does every female," I said.

"Well, yes." Dad cleared his throat. "A steer is a bull that's been altered. This is to say, his glands of reproduction have been removed. When a stallion is altered, or gelded, as they say of horses, he is called a gelding."

"I understand," I said. So now I knew what steers were.

While this question-and-answer session had been going on, the foreman had been driving west across the pasture. It was a bumpy enough ride, but nothing to what was in store for us. Dad jumped out to open another gate, and suddenly we were headed into the heart of the hills.

There was no road, not even a fire trail. We just went along ledges which time and erosion had carved out of the hillsides. I was almost as scared as when I first got on Sam. I tried to hang onto the side of the jeep as it bucked and rattled over rocks and fallen oak limbs. We plunged down a canyon that didn't seem to have any bottom, then up a slope that reached to the sky. Now and then we came to a level, open glade and I was aware of wild flowers everywhere. Poppies, owl's clover, shooting stars, and buttercups. I suppose it was all very pretty. Only I couldn't enjoy it.

"How much farther do we have to go?" I asked Mr. Railey, who seemed to be thoroughly enjoying a chance to put the jeep through its paces.

"I'm not sure," was his consoling answer. "We've got twenty thousand acres in this ranch and the darned horses might be in any part of it."

On we went, higher and higher, and then the oaks parted, and suddenly, looking down, I saw the horses in a small meadow right below us.

"There they are," I cried.

"Hold on," yelled the foreman, and the next thing I knew, he had guided the jeep right off that ledge and straight down the hillside. I was sure we were going to tip over, and it flashed through my mind that it would make a colorful headline in the local paper: FATHER AND DAUGHTER KILLED IN FALL FROM JEEP WHILE CHASING WILD STALLION. It never occurred to me that the foreman would be killed, too. Chuck Railey seemed too durable for that.

As we approached the green meadow where the horses were grazing, the foreman slowed down. By the time we had emerged from the trees at its edge, we were crawling. Mr. Railey turned off the motor and swung out of the jeep.

"You two stay where you are," he ordered.

He reached into the jeep and from somewhere around Dad's feet pulled out a halter. Then, moving very quietly, he approached the horses.

There were eight of them. Seven had foals at their sides. They barely noticed us. But the eighth horse, the stallion, was approaching where the jeep was parked, moving so that he came between the mares and the man on foot.

That stallion was the most beautiful thing I have ever seen. For the first time in my life I wished I weren't afraid of horses. I honestly wanted not to be afraid of him. He was so lovely. I heard Dad say under his breath, "God, what a horse." He had taken the words right out of my mouth.

To begin with, he was the color of the bottom of Mom's copper-bottomed pots right after she has polished them. (Which she doesn't do very often.) His wavy mane rippled down to his withers, and his tail, also wavy, brushed the ground. They, too, shone like polished copper. There was a white star between his eyes and a white strip running down his nose. His two back legs were white a little way up.

He walked powerfully, and you could see his muscles working under his satiny hide. He stopped, flung up his head, and snorted.

Mr. Railey halted in his tracks, and the two studied each other for about half a minute. Then the man went forward slowly again and the stallion held his ground. Slowly, slowly, Mr. Railey drew nearer to him. When he was close enough, he put out a hand and gently laid it on the stallion's neck. You could see the horse quiver, but he never moved away. Then the man stepped closer, put the halter strap around the stallion's neck, and waited a moment. Next he moved the nose piece toward the stallion's nostrils. To my amazement, the horse dipped his head and Mr. Railey slipped the halter over his nose and fastened the halter strap. He turned toward us. "You can come now. Move slowly."

Dad got quietly down from the jeep, and so did I. We went carefully toward the little meadow and paused about twenty feet away from where Mr. Railey stood holding the stallion. He made a gesture toward the mares.

"There's his 'get,'" he said.

"They're fine-looking foals," Dad replied.

Evidently, "get" meant the foals a stallion sired.

"He's halter-broke," Mr. Railey explained, "but he hasn't had one on him for months, and I wasn't sure he'd take it." As he spoke he was stroking the underside of the stallion's neck.

"What's his name?" I asked.

"This is Aranaway Ethan. Great-grandson of the great Mansfield. Even has Mansfield's white fetlocks."

I had been so struck with Aranaway Ethan's beauty that I hadn't had eyes for anything else. Now I looked over at Dad. Never have I seen such an expression on his face.

Every now and then in my missalette at church I have come across the word "exalted." I've known more or less what it means. But I had never felt the real honest sense of it until I saw Dad's face as he stood there looking at that stallion. His expression was a mixture of joy and awe. His eyes were misty, and I realized all at once that never in his whole life had he hoped to possess a horse like this one. Right then I would have willingly mounted that stallion and let him toss me as high as the oak trees if that was the only way Dad could get to keep him.

"Come on over," Mr. Railey said to Dad. "He's

relaxed now. He's not afraid of people. Actually, he's got a real nice disposition. Typical Morgan disposition. Trouble is, no one's ever done anything with him."

Dad went toward Aranaway Ethan and laid a hand on his neck. He patted him gently. Then, stooping, he ran a hand down his nearest front leg. He did the same with a back leg. The horse never moved.

"Is it correct that you're asking three hundred dollars for him?" Dad asked.

"Yep. He's worth that, dead or alive."

Dad looked at Mr. Railey questioningly.

"He's worth three hundred dollars as horse meat."

Dad looked shocked, and I said, "Oh, no!"

Mr. Railey looked over at me and shook his head. "He's not good for anything else unless someone takes him and trains him."

"I'll take him," said Dad.

He moved around the stallion and ran his hand down his other legs. "His cannon bones are clean."

Mr. Railey nodded. "He's sound. You can have him vetted, of course. But at the price, you're not taking much of a chance. I'll show you his papers when we get back to the ranch. He's seven years old. This spring."

The foreman slipped the halter off Aranaway Ethan, gave him a friendly slap on the rump, and the stallion went snorting off toward the mares.

"What do you think of him, Melinda? He's going to be your horse, you know."

"He won't be my horse for a long time, Dad. And that's okay with me. He's just got to be the most beautiful horse in the world. And I'm glad you're going to buy him. I couldn't bear to have him turned into horse meat."

On the way back to the ranch, Dad and the foreman arranged to have the stallion delivered to our barn. Dad asked about a vet to geld him, and Mr. Railey was very helpful with all kinds of information. I had dreaded our ride back, but it wasn't nearly so rough as our ride out because now we didn't have to look into every canyon and out from every ridge for horses.

Dad wrote out a check for Aranaway Ethan, pocketed his papers, and we drove back home.

"I'll send the papers in to the Morgan Association tomorrow so they can change the ownership of Aranaway Ethan from Granite Ranch to Melinda

Ross," Dad explained on the way. "Now at last you own a horse, Melinda. And a mighty fine one. What do you say we drop the 'Aranaway' and just call him Ethan?"

"It's okay with me," I replied. "I don't much like the sound of that 'Aranaway' anyway."

"That's just the name of the breeding farm he came from."

"Oh," I said, thankful that it didn't indicate a special characteristic of this horse "we" had bought.

4

The Good Luck Horse

Dad had arranged with Mr. Railey to have Ethan delivered to our barn on the following Saturday. Meanwhile, he and I spent a lot of time cleaning up that old rookery. It was full of cobwebs and assorted junk. In the short time we'd been living here, he hadn't had time to do much about getting it in shape. But now that a horse was actually going to be in it, Dad was in a frenzy to have it as ready as could be.

Naturally I helped. Not that I wanted to. But since we came home together every afternoon, I couldn't just sit around while he was down at the barn working his head off. Helping Dad, I discovered a funny thing about myself. I simply loathe housework. Dusting is the most boring occupation I can even imagine. But I got a kick out of cleaning the barn. Maybe it was because it was so dirty to begin with you could take some satisfaction in seeing what you accomplished. Mom is a perfect housekeeper, and I can't see that the living room looks any different after I've spent the better part of half an hour dusting it than it did before I started. But a half hour swinging a broom around that barn made a real difference.

There were three oversize box stalls with mangers. These had been chewed along their edges by generations of horses. A paddock the length of the barn extended out from the barn for about fifty feet. There was a water faucet in one corner, and under the faucet was an old bathtub sitting on claw feet.

Over the years the boards of the barn had shrunk in places, letting in sunlight that made the dust motes dance. There were some holes in the roof.

After about the fourth day, Dad stood looking around at our handiwork, his expression deeply satisfied.

"Well, it's not Morgan Manor," he said, "but with a board here and a shingle there, it will make Ethan

a very good shelter from wind and sun and rain."
He moved into the middle stall. "We'll board up the
sides of this and use it for hay and tack. I'll fix some
racks for saddles and bridles."

"How many saddles do you intend to have? And
bridles?"

He looked a little sheepish. "Just one of each right
now. And I'll have to start inquiring around for a
saddle. A second-hand one won't cost as much as a
new one, and it has the advantage of being broken
in. Maybe Dodge Rayburn will have one. We'll get
the bridle new." He leveled a finger at me. "And it
will be your job to keep the tack clean."

I didn't say anything, knowing it would be some
time before Ethan would be sweating up a saddle.

We'd had rain off and on all week, but Saturday
was as clear and bright as you could wish. Mr.
Railey had phoned to say he'd arrive around ten,
and at ten the Ross family was out on the front lawn
looking west down the Estates road. You couldn't
see far because the road sloped so steeply down.

Mom had left her baking and stood on the front
porch of the old house, her eyes fixed on the road.
Dad paced back and forth over the lawn, getting his
feet wet. I felt excited, too, as I joined Mom on the
porch.

50

Since Mom and I were above the lawn, we saw it first. "Here they come," we cried together, and then we could hear the truck toiling up the grade. Now it was in sight, a big pickup, and pulling a two-horse trailer. Dad ran out to the edge of the road and motioned toward our driveway. Mr. Railey was all alone. He slowly and carefully turned the truck into our driveway and, with Dad running alongside, started down toward the barn. Mom and I hurried off the porch after them.

Mr. Railey descended from the truck cab, and Dad introduced him to Mom.

"Before I unload him I'd like a look around," Mr. Railey said to Dad. He followed Dad to the barn. As soon as he saw the paddock, he asked, "Is there an outside gate to that paddock?"

"Yes," Dad answered.

"Good. Because I don't think I could get the stallion to go into the barn too soon. He's used to being out. But he'll go into the paddock without any trouble."

We all four went outside again, and Mr. Railey opened the window of the trailer up front where Ethan was tied. Ethan instantly put his head out and snorted.

"Oh, Cal," said Mom, "what a beautiful head."

"True Morgan," said Dad.

All at once there was a cry from the direction of the driveway. "Hi, Melinda," yelled Diana. "We saw the horse trailer go by and knew it was your horse."

Dwight was with her.

It was the first time since we'd moved here that Dwight had been at our house. And it was the horse that had brought him!

Mom introduced them to Mr. Railey in a kind of offhand way, but Dwight stepped right up and shook hands. Very manly.

"Glad to meet you," said Mr. Railey. "We may be able to use an extra hand before we get this fellow unloaded."

Dwight's as big as a man and heavy without being fat. Just strong-looking. I knew better than to pay any attention to him and of course he never even looked at me; he never does. What boy of fifteen would know that his kid sister's best friend is even alive? Just the same, I thought Dwight looked and acted real neat that morning beside the trailer.

Mr. Railey got into the cab of the pickup after closing Ethan's window and very slowly drove toward the paddock gate beyond the barn. He turned the truck in a wide circle, then began carefully backing it toward the gate. It took a while to maneuver it into position. Meanwhile, Dad had opened the gate, and Mr. Railey backed the trailer almost up to it. He turned off the motor and went around to the back of the trailer.

"How did you ever get the stallion into that trailer?" Dad asked.

I was wondering about the same thing.

Mr. Railey began opening the back of the trailer. You could see Ethan's copper-colored rump above the doors.

"First I tranquilized him," he said, "and then with two guys helping me, we got him into a chute that led right up to the back end of the trailer. He went in without too much trouble. He sort of trusts people," he added.

Before he went around to open the back doors, Mr. Railey had opened the window by Ethan's head and unsnapped the rope that tied him to the trailer. Next he snapped a lead rope onto the halter and tossed it over Ethan's neck. As soon as he had opened the back doors he came around front again and, reaching through the window, took hold of Ethan's halter. He started gently pushing him backward. All the time he was talking quietly to him. "Back, boy, back. It's okay. Back up." Slowly Ethan began to move backward. When his feet hit the slatted, sloping ramp leading from the trailer to the ground, he banged around a bit. But now Dad and Mr. Railey were both there, urging him to "Back, boy, back." And after only a brief struggle on the ramp, Ethan sort of skidded onto the ground inside the paddock. Instantly Mr. Railey grabbed the lead rope on the stallion's neck. Ethan had been unloaded! Now he was really and truly ours.

"Mr. Railey," Mom called from outside the paddock where we three were standing. "I have something for Ethan."

Sometimes I think my Mom has more sense than any of us. While I had been watching the whole unloading process, she had run to the house, and now here she was with a carrot in her hand!

"May I give him this?" she called.

Mr. Railey grinned. "I can see right now how it's going to be. He's hardly got his feet on the ground and already you're starting to spoil him."

"Surely giving him a reward for being so good about coming out of that trailer wouldn't be spoiling him!" Mom protested.

Mr. Railey shrugged and grinned. "Have it your own way; he's your horse. But I go by the old saying, 'Never do a horse a favor.' "

Dad said, backing Mom up, "Oh, I'm not so sure of that. It depends a lot on the horse. I think it won't hurt Ethan to know we're glad to have him here."

Mr. Railey led Ethan over to the fence. He looked so beautiful in the spring sunshine! He was almost as bright as the poppies showing on the green hill across the road.

Mom broke off a piece of carrot, stepped up onto a lower board of the paddock fence, and held out her hand, the palm flat, with the carrot resting on it. Ethan bowed his head and sniffed the carrot. But he didn't take it. It was plain he had never seen a carrot before. Mom kept her hand out and again he sniffed the carrot. He backed off a step. Finally, reaching out, he lifted the piece of carrot off her hand and began eating it. She broke off another piece, and this time he took it right away.

"Spoiled already," said Mr. Railey, but he looked pleased. "From now on every time he sees you, he'll be expecting a handout."

"And getting it," said Mom.

Mr. Railey led Ethan to the middle of the paddock and made him stand a certain way, lifting his head high and moving the stallion forward so that his hind feet were stretched way back and his front feet were exactly in line with each other.

"Look at that!" exclaimed Dad. "He practically stretched himself."

That's how I learned what it meant to "stretch" a horse.

Mr. Railey called out to Dad, "I think I'd leave his halter on for a few days. Let him get used to it."

He unsnapped the lead rope, stood back, and Ethan took off, bucking and kicking. He held his tail straight up above his rump, the long hairs trailing down from it. His neck was arched as he tore around the paddock. Then he skidded to a stop in a cloud of dust, threw up his head, and snorted.

"Goodness!" exclaimed Mom. "Do you really think you'll ever tame him, Cal?"

"Sure," Dad answered. "Once he's gelded, a lot of that steam will go out of him."

Mr. Railey pulled the trailer out of the paddock, and Dad fastened the gate. I could see now that there was a bale of hay in the pickup. Dad, Mom, Dwight, and I followed the pickup to where it stopped in front of the barn.

"I brought you a bale of alfalfa," said Mr. Railey,

getting down from the truck. "Where do you want to put it?"

"I appreciate that," said Dad. "I'll take care of it."

He started for the pickup, but Dwight was ahead of him. I don't think I've ever been so proud of anybody in my life. Before Dad hardly knew what was happening, Dwight was in that pickup and, with two hay hooks that he must have found on the bed of the truck, was wrestling the bale toward the tailgate. Mr. Railey opened it, and Dwight shoved the bale of hay to the ground. He jumped down after it.

"Where do you want me to put it, Mr. Ross?"

"Melinda will show you," Dad told him. "Thanks, Dwight."

So with me leading and Dwight coming along behind, the heavy bale of alfalfa banging against his knees, we started for the barn. Once inside I pointed to the middle stall.

"Anywhere in there," I said.

Dwight shoved the bale into place, took the hay hooks out of it, and turned toward me. His job was finished, but I just couldn't, I simply couldn't, let it all end like that. This was the very first time we had ever been alone together.

"My, but you're strong, Dwight."

I could tell by the disgusted way he looked at me that I had said something utterly dumb. It even occurred to me in a flash that he might think that I thought he had been showing off to me. As if he ever would! Maybe he had been showing off before the two grown men. But he sure wouldn't bother to show off to me.

Then while I was thinking all this, I saw a different look come into his face. His eyes, which had been staring at me as if I were some kind of slug, lost their disgust and something almost like a smile moved his lips.

"You're not a bad kid," he said. "Someday you'll grow up and get some sense."

He brushed past me and the next moment was out of the barn. I just stood there in a kind of daze. Dwight had actually looked at me! He had said I was a good kid!

A shadow fell across the door into the paddock. I turned. There was Ethan. He snorted slightly and stuck his head in.

"Oh, Ethan," I cried, starting toward him. "You're a really, truly good-luck horse."

Ethan sprang back and galloped away.

5

Changes

As I look back on it now, my life changed quite a bit after the Saturday morning Ethan came to live with us. I was still Melinda Ross, tall for ten, curly hair worn in a pigtail because it's easier to comb curly hair when you keep it braided, with sort of ordinary green eyes and a mouth I think is too big for my face. (Dad says it indicates a generous nature.) But from that Saturday on, life was definitely changed for me.

To begin with, every morning right after breakfast I had to go out and feed Ethan. Dad had shown me how much of the alfalfa hay to give him. This wasn't hard to do because the hay was pressed flat and you just lifted off the amount you wanted and carried it to him. Ethan wouldn't go into the barn at first, so I had to take it out to the paddock and throw it on the ground for him. In a couple of days he was standing with his head in the barn door when I entered, and at sight of me he nickered. I always said, "Hi, Ethan," and when I approached him with the hay in my arms, he always backed out and waited quietly for me to give it to him. Then I had to check the bathtub to make sure there was plenty of water in it. Usually I drained out the water that was there and added fresh.

Beyond making up my bed, I had never had any chores to do before school. But now I had to care for Ethan because Dad didn't have time in the morning. When you have to go to work at five-thirty, you don't have time to fool around with horses.

Mom had offered to take on this chore herself, but Dad wouldn't let her.

"He's Melinda's horse, and if Melinda is ever to get to know him, she's got to be around him. And the sooner the quicker."

"But, Cal, isn't a stallion too dangerous for a child to be around?" Mom had argued.

"Some stallions, yes. This stallion is a Morgan,

and a very gentle Morgan at that. I don't want her handling him until he's gelded. But she's taking no risk in feeding him."

Mom said no more, trusting to Dad's judgment as she always does, and I had a new duty to perform.

Of course, having to take care of Ethan every day made me less and less afraid of him. Just as Dad knew it would. And now that Ethan was nickering to me every time he saw me, I began to develop a special feeling about him. It was as if there were an understanding between us that he didn't have with anybody else, even Dad. I began to want to hang around the paddock in the afternoons when Dad was handling him. This handling took the form of snapping the rope to the stallion's halter and leading him around and around the paddock. Then Dad would drop the rope and let it hang while he tried to pick up one of Ethan's front feet. He would carefully run his hand down the leg, pinching a little just above the fetlock. Sometimes Ethan would lift his foot, and sometimes he wouldn't. But Dad always kept at it until he finally did lift it. Then Dad would scrape across it lightly with a hoof pick and set it down again. Always he patted Ethan afterward.

For another change in my life, I wasn't watching nearly as much TV as I had before. I was too busy watching Dad and Ethan. I didn't worry about this because there's nothing much on in the late afternoon but talk shows. Mostly people you never heard of talking about themselves. Pretty boring. But even on Saturday I was out at the paddock.

I suppose it's only natural that when you take on anything as big as a horse, it's bound to crowd some other things out of your life.

And then, of course, there was Missy. We would never have known Missy if it hadn't been for Ethan. And Missy is one of the most important things that has happened to me so far. More about that later.

The Thursday following Ethan's arrival, Dad announced at dinner, "Tomorrow the vet will be here to geld Ethan."

"Can I watch?" I asked.

"Oh, no, Melinda," said Mom. "I hardly think so."

"Why not?" asked Dad. "There's nothing mysterious or particularly gory about it. A very simple operation, really. If she's going to be a horsewoman, she's got to know as much as she can about horses. Gelding a stallion is a very ordinary aspect of horse husbandry."

Mom said no more, and the next afternoon I was on hand to watch what was going to happen. Dr. Vance arrived in a special pickup full of built-in cases to hold medicine and instruments. He turned out to be tall and broad-shouldered. He spoke quietly and moved about as if he knew his business. He asked Dad to bring Ethan out onto our lawn, where he would perform the operation.

"I'll tranquilize him first," he said. "Then when we get him onto the lawn I'll anesthetize him."

The two men went into the paddock. Ethan had found his way into the barn by now. Dad went in and snapped the lead rope onto Ethan's halter. The stallion allowed the vet to approach. Quickly Dr. Vance stuck a hypodermic needle into Ethan's neck, and the stallion winced. The lead rope now had a chain on it that went over Ethan's nose from the place where it was snapped to the halter. By pulling down on the chain, Dad had good command over him. Next the vet attached the barrel of the syringe to the hypodermic needle and shot the tranquilizer into Ethan. We waited a few minutes for it to take effect, and then Dr. Vance signaled Dad to lead the stallion out. Ethan went very quietly and for once didn't fling his head up and snort.

Meanwhile, Dr. Vance's assistant, a young woman almost as sturdily built as he was, had laid out all the instruments and cotton and towels and stuff that the vet would need.

Dad led Ethan over to where she was waiting. The vet took another hypodermic needle from the assistant's hand and again stuck it into Ethan's neck. This time he didn't even wince.

Now there was no waiting for the shot to take effect. Almost immediately Ethan's four feet buckled together and he was down and on his side. Quickly Dr. Vance tied a rope around his neck in a nonslip knot. He jerked the rope several times to make sure it wouldn't slip. Then he paid out enough to tie part of it around Ethan's top hind fetlock. Next he drew up the stallion's leg until his hoof was resting against his neck, exposing the place to be operated on. Dr. Vance drew the other end of the rope through the loop around Ethan's neck, and the assistant took hold of it.

Dr. Vance knelt beside Ethan. Before I hardly knew what was happening, it was all over and the vet was putting antibiotic into the open wounds where the glands had been removed. He got to his feet.

"He'll be out for a few more minutes," he said, looking down at Ethan.

Now the assistant untied the rope from Ethan's foot and placed a towel over his eyes.

"That makes it a little easier for him when he wakes up," the vet explained. "They seem less confused when they wake up with their eyes darkened."

While Dad and Dr. Vance talked, I just stood there looking down at Ethan. Suddenly I felt terribly, terribly sorry for him. This magnificent animal, so spirited, so full of life, lay there like so much helpless flesh. Would our high-headed, high-stepping Aranaway Ethan ever come back to us? I felt tears sting my eyes and wiped them away furiously. Imagine me crying over a horse!

"Will he ever be the way he was before?" I asked Dr. Vance.

I couldn't keep a catch out of my voice, and the big man put an arm around me.

"Don't worry, kiddo. By tomorrow you won't know I ever touched him. He'll even have a good appetite for dinner tonight." He looked over at Dad. "Starting tomorrow morning, you'll have to walk him around a lot. That's to prevent a blood clot forming."

"How soon will it be safe for Melinda to handle him?" Dad asked.

"You can start training him any day now. But I wouldn't want this little girl working with him for a couple of months. It takes longer for the hormones to get out of an older horse's system than it would a very young stallion. But after a couple of months he shouldn't be showing any stallion aggressiveness at all."

Two months! I wouldn't be expected ˙to get aboard Ethan for two months! What a relief! But almost immediately I realized that I couldn't ride him anyway until he was trained. And surely it would take at least two months to make Ethan into the reliable, responsive mount that Dad had in mind for me.

Suddenly Ethan raised his head off the lawn and the towel fell to one side. He heaved himself to a sitting-up position, then thrust his front legs straight out in front of him, pushed his hind legs under him, and rose to his feet. He stood for a moment with his head down and his feet spread. Dr. Vance's assistant undid the rope around his neck. As Dad reached for the lead rope still fastened to his halter, Ethan raised his head and looked around him. Then he lowered it to the grass at his feet and began cropping! The gelding was over.

I was sure Mom would let me off dusting next morning so I could watch Dad walking Ethan. After all, he was my horse, and I was naturally interested in how he was getting along after his operation. I hadn't been out to the barn yet, as Dad does the morning feeding on weekends. Now that Ethan was going in and out of the barn, we fed him there. That meant his stall had to be mucked out. Dad did this each day when he came off his route. Saturday mornings he did a more thorough job.

"Since Dad has to walk Ethan this morning, I thought I'd muck the barn out for him."

"I'm sure he'll appreciate that," said Mom, reaching into a cupboard for a mixing bowl. "Why don't you go and tell him you'll be out to help as soon as you've finished your housework?"

"I thought maybe if I was helping Dad, you'd let me off the housework for one morning."

She began breaking eggs into the bowl. "You may as well understand right now, Melinda, that that horse is not going to get in the way of your responsibilities here and at school. Your father wants you to be a good horsewoman, and I think that's fine. But I want you to grow up knowing a few useful things. Like learning to manage a house along with whatever other career you may choose for yourself." She took a can of frozen strawberries and a carton of whipping cream out of the refrigerator. I could see it was going to be a strawberry-whip cream cake. My favorite. "Besides," she continued, "I work very hard all week and I can do with a little help on Saturday. I'm sure you feel as I do that that's only fair in exchange for your allowance."

I get three dollars a week.

I walked out of the kitchen without saying anything. I felt in my bones she was right, and after all, she was going to the trouble of making us a strawberry-whip cream cake. But I was in such a bad mood that I wasn't about to let that fact sweeten my dusting.

So later, when she poked her head around the living room door and asked, "Do you want to lick off the beaters?" I put on my most sullen expression and answered rudely, "No."

"Thank you," added Mom sweetly, and I felt about five years old.

Once I knocked my knuckles hard on a corner of the mantel over the fireplace. It hurt and I said, "Damn," good and loud. No scolding came from the kitchen. Maybe she hadn't heard me.

Suddenly as I was dusting the circular rungs of the cane-backed rocker, I straightened up to stare out the window at the hills across the road. A March wind was flattening the grass on their slopes, and the sky looked like rain. A thought had just struck me.

Though at the start of my spat with Mom I had only wanted to get out of dusting, as my sulk had continued I realized I honestly did want to know how Ethan was. I couldn't understand why I hadn't run out to the barn the minute I came downstairs before breakfast. It just hadn't entered my head to do it. I knew in my heart of hearts he was all right or Dad would have said something before now. Still, I felt I had to know. I dropped my dust cloth and went into the kitchen.

"Do you care if I run out to see if Ethan is okay? I'll come right back and finish dusting."

Mom looked up and smiled. "That will please your dad."

I ran out the kitchen across the old-fashioned screened back porch, letting the screen door slam behind me. Off across the yard I could see Dad walking Ethan around and around the paddock. I climbed up on the paddock fence.

"How is he?" I called.

Dad walked him over, and I pulled a piece of carrot out of my jeans and offered it to Ethan. He took it at once.

"He's fine," said Dad. "Quiet as can be."

"I'll be back to muck out the stall as soon as I've finished dusting."

"That won't be necessary, honey. I'll have lots of time to do it between walkings."

"No, I want to, he's my horse. If I can't walk him, then the least I can do is clean up after him."

"Okay, have it your way," he said as he started Ethan up again. He looked really pleased.

I went back and finished the dusting. Then I went into the kitchen where Mom was filling the cake shell with the strawberry-whip cream mixture.

"Did you rinse off the beaters?"

She pointed to where they lay on the counter. I could see she had left a lot of whipped cream on them. It looked as if she had hardly shaken them at all.

I licked the beaters clean, wiped my face off on a paper towel, and returned to the barn. I had already changed the beds.

Interruption

I don't know what to call the next few pages, so, since they interrupt this story, I will just call them an interruption.

After I had finished the last chapter, I decided to show what I had done to Missy. She read it, pencil in hand, while I played with Fancy, her white whippet. I sort of kept my eye on her, and now and then she made a mark with the pencil. It took her quite a while to read it all because I could see she was reading it carefully, not skimming over it the way most grown-ups read what a kid has written.

When she had finished, she laid the manuscript

down on her lap, snatched off her glasses, and said, "Melinda, I'm impressed. You're a natural-born writer, and I think you should give up any idea you may still be entertaining about being an airline stewardess."

Well, of course I felt pretty excited at hearing this because I had discovered as this book went along that I liked writing. I've never been too crazy about reading; I've always preferred to watch TV. Maybe it was just living over again the events of the happiest year of my life so far (and in one particular way, the saddest) that made writing about it seem fun. Certainly it's been the most interesting year I ever lived. But maybe the years get more interesting as you get older. I don't know.

But to get back to Missy and this interruption.

"I like the way you're telling your story," she went on. "It sounds exactly like you. But better than anything is the way you see into yourself and describe how you feel about what is happening." She flipped over a few pages. "I've marked what I thought was an awkward passage here and there and cleaned up some of your spelling. But don't you dare let me or anybody else tell you how to write this book. It's your very own and it's unique."

I didn't know what that meant, but I made a note to look it up at school. We don't own a dictionary.

I had been making good use of the school dictionary. Right away when I began this book, I discovered that it sounded boring to use "said" over and over again. So I made a list of all the words you could use instead of "said." There's quite a lot of them. I made lists of adjectives and adverbs, too.

When I told Missy about this the day she read my story, she said, "But, dear child, the best way to build a vocabulary is by reading. I never knew a writer who wasn't a reader."

The next time she came to our house she had an armload of books for me. I must say she's a good picker and I liked all of them except one which she said was a favorite of hers when she was a little girl. It was called *Little Women*. It's been over sixty years since Missy was a little girl, and I guess you can't expect her to know without fail what a modern girl likes. Though I must say Missy comes very close to it. And it's just not possible to think of her as old.

Mom said one day after we'd known Missy for a couple of months, "That woman has convinced me that old age is a state of mind."

I think Missy would agree with that. She says her

motto is: "As long as I can, I will."

There were two reasons why I wanted Missy to read these first five chapters. First, I was curious to know if I was on the right track with this book and if it was worthwhile to continue with it. Missy definitely thinks it's worthwhile. Second, this is the only part of the book I can let her see because from now on she is in it. I knew, if I thought she was going to be reading what I had written about her, I would sort of hold back on what I wanted to say. It wasn't that I was going to say anything bad about her (you couldn't say anything bad about Missy), but I felt shy about letting her see how important she had become to me. I know she will never ask to see the rest of it. Missy is the kind of person who is always interested in what you are doing, but not curious about it. There's a great difference between the two.

So now I'll go on with my story, encouraged that Missy thinks it's good so far.

6

Missy

Up to now I haven't said much about what people look like in this book. Not even my parents. But then, all parents look pretty much alike. Some are fat and some are thin. But they're all about the same age, and wear about the same kind of clothes and expressions.

Now, however, I am going to take time out to describe Missy. In the first place, that isn't her name. She's really Muriel Zinn. That's the name she writes under. It wasn't long after we got acquainted with her that she and Dad and Mom were calling each other by their first names. But

Mom didn't think it was right for me to call her Muriel, because she is so old.

"It just isn't dignified for a girl of ten to be calling a woman in her seventies by her first name," Mom said.

Missy tried to persuade Mom to let me, but Mom stood firm as she is apt to do when it is a question of manners.

So for the first few weeks I called her Miss Zinn. But as we got to know each other better and better, I shortened that to Miss Z. And in no time at all I had shortened that to Missy. This pleased her, and since she disliked her first name, she begged Dad and Mom to call her Missy, too. And so she became Missy to our family.

She is small; hardly taller than I am. Her normal weight is around one hundred and five. She's wiry but not stringy, and she doesn't look her age. She wears her gray hair cut very short and shaped around her head like a helmet, with bangs across her forehead. She manages to keep a good suntan all the year around. Her face is heavily lined, of course, but her skin fits close over the bones of her face. There is no sign of a double chin, though her neck is stringy. Naturally.

It's her eyes, though, that you really look at. I have never seen eyes like Missy's. They are exactly the color of violets, and when she wants to turn it on, they have a peculiar light in them, as if she knew a marvelous secret she was dying to share. At the same time, her mouth gets a little quirk in it at one corner. At these moments, just looking at her makes a strange excitement start growing in you. A lot of the time there is good cause for excitement. Missy has a way of making things happen. Her voice is a little on the husky side, pitched low. She listens as much as she talks. You can't say that about most old ladies. My grandmother who lives in New York talks all the time. The last time she came to visit us, Dad said someone should throw a cover over her cage. It made Mom mad and you can't really blame her. She's Mom's mother. She's all the grandparents I have. Fortunately.

Missy isn't a bit like any other old lady you're ever likely to know.

It makes me smile now to think that the first time I saw Missy I detested her. I thought her a silly old fool and a meddler.

I'll never forget that first meeting. It was on the morning of the second Saturday following the gelding. Dad and I were marking out the space for a riding ring. It would be ninety feet wide and a hundred and twenty feet long. Since he had paid so little for Ethan, he had decided he could afford a few extras, like turning some of our three acres into a ring. The exciting thing about it for me was that he asked Dwight to help him dig the holes for the fence posts. Dwight was coming over this afternoon and every Saturday afternoon until the ring was finished. I intended to be there helping as much as I could.

We had just got nicely started with our measuring when a sporty little red car came zooming up our driveway. A gray-haired woman quickly got out of it and started across the backyard to where we were working.

"Are you Mr. Ross?" she asked when she had got within speaking distance of us.

"Yes, I am," Dad answered.

She walked straight up to him without any hesitation and put out her hand. "I'm Muriel Zinn. Dodge Rayburn thought you might be able to help me since you own a Morgan." For a moment her violet eyes rested on me while she gave me the friendliest smile you could imagine.

"My daughter, Melinda," said Dad.

"Hi, Melinda," she said, turning back to Dad.

"I'm looking for a Morgan gelding. Mr. Rayburn thought you might know of one."

Dad shook his head slowly. "Not offhand," he said.

Missy frowned at the ground, then lifted her head. "I've been doing some inquiring around. Do you have a minute?"

Dad nodded.

"I'll make it short," she went on. "For the first time in my life I have the leisure and the money for a horse. It takes both, you know."

Dad grinned. "I know!"

"Well, at my age one can't be sure that riding is the thing one really should do. I rode a lot when I was young. But I rode Western. And now I want to ride English. I'm not sure how good a rider I'll be. So I thought that instead of buying a horse right away, I would try to lease one. I thought maybe you'd be able to help me find one. And give me riding lessons."

"Well, Mrs. Zinn . . ." Dad began.

She corrected him quickly. "Miss Zinn."

"Sorry, Miss Zinn. I suppose I could find time to

give you lessons if you succeed in finding a horse. Does it have to be a Morgan?"

"Yes, it does." She sounded very sure. "Ever since I watched a Morgan show back in Massachusetts thirty years ago, my heart has been set on a Morgan."

"You have good taste in horses," said Dad. "Our Morgan belongs to Melinda. Would you care to see him?"

"Oh, *please*," she answered, and her husky voice had a special note in it.

"Call out your horse, Melinda," Dad said.

Ethan had learned to go into the barn now. We didn't confine him to his stall because Dad had sided up the tack stall and kept its door slid shut so Ethan couldn't get at the hay stored there. I climbed through the paddock fence bars and went over to the barn door.

"Hi, Ethan," I called. Right away his head came poking out for a look around.

"Oh, he's lovely," said Miss Zinn. "How I'd love to have one just like him!"

Ethan knew by this time that I always had a carrot in my pocket for him and now I broke off a piece and held it toward him. He came straight to me and took it gently off my hand.

While Dad told her the story of how we got him, I patted him and smoothed his nose just as if I'd been around horses all my life and didn't want to be anywhere else.

Dad mentioned Morgan Manor.

"I've already been there," said Miss Zinn. "They don't lease horses. But they told me about a Morgan show to be held at Woodside next Saturday and suggested I might talk to some of the exhibitors there." Suddenly she got that look in her eyes. "Why couldn't we all go to Woodside? Would you like that, Melinda?"

All at once I felt fury rising in me. One glance told me that Dad was as happy as could be at the idea of going to one more Morgan horse show. But Dwight was coming next Saturday to help dig postholes. How could we just take off and let him do it all by himself with no one to give him ice-cold Cokes as I had planned to do this afternoon? Even if Mom stayed home, Dad would expect me to go because I was to become this great horsewoman. Anything to do with horses and I was supposed to be there with both feet. Well, I wasn't going to go, and that was final.

So I looked this meddling old woman straight in the eye and without a trace of regret in my voice said, "We can't go. We're building a riding ring and a man is coming to help us this afternoon and next Saturday and we have to be here, my father and I. And my mother wouldn't be the least bit interested in going," I added for good measure.

I saw the light go out of the old woman's eyes as she turned them to Dad in a questioning way.

"For Heaven's sake, Melinda, where did you get that crazy idea?" he said, as if he couldn't believe his ears. "Of course we'll go. What on earth needs to keep us home?"

"Like I said. Dwight will be working and who'll give him his Cokes?"

"If that's all, we'll give him a key to the back door and he can help himself."

"I know Mom won't want to go. She has too much to do on Saturday. And if she stays home, I'm going to stay home with her."

By this time Missy could see that I was really furious and teed off at her.

"Well!" she said, letting her breath out on the word. "I didn't mean to start a family ruckus. I just assumed that a girl who owned such a beautiful Morgan would look forward to a Morgan show. Any Morgan show."

"And so she should," said Dad. "And so she shall. Unless my wife decides not to go, we'll all three be delighted to join you for the Woodside show."

I threw the metal measuring tape I had been holding onto the ground and burst into tears. I know it was a dumb thing to do, but I was so mad I couldn't hold in another minute. For the first time in my life I was impertinent to my father, and before a stranger, too. I never once thought of Martin.

"You can't make me look forward to it and I'm not going to be delighted about it," I fairly shouted. Then I ran to the house.

As usual Mom was in the kitchen doing the Saturday baking.

"What on earth's the matter?" she cried as I came storming in.

"There's a hateful old woman out there who's talked Dad into going to a Morgan show in Woodside next Saturday. And I'm not going."

"Of course you're going if he wants you to." She went calmly on about her business. "Unless, of course, you're ill, and then you'll have to stay in bed all day and I'll stay home to take care of you." She crossed to the sink and ran some water into a mixing bowl. "Why don't you want to go? I was beginning to think you were starting to take an interest in horses."

"I don't want to, that's all."

"Not a very good reason," she said.

Suddenly a thought struck me, and she had just given me the idea for it.

"It's because I *am* getting interested in horses that I want to stay home. I want to work on the ring with Dwight."

"That's what I thought," said Mom, turning around from the sink and leaning against it. "Melinda, I hate to say this, but you are being a very silly little girl. I have no criticism of your having a crush on a boy so much older than you that he is scarcely aware of your existence. I remember when I was in the fourth grade there was an eighth-grade boy I thought was the most wonderful thing on earth. But I was smart enough not to let anyone know about it, including the boy. You are simply making yourself ridiculous."

She tore off a paper towel and wiped her hands. "Growing up is the toughest thing that will ever happen to you, dear. It won't get any easier for the next ten years." She opened the cupboard door under the sink and threw the dampened towel into the garbage bag there. "As for Dwight, your Dad and I both think he is a very fine boy and will grow into a very fine man. I don't blame you for liking him; we all like him. And there's no reason to think he dislikes you because he pays no attention to you. After all, you're just his kid sister's friend. But he will begin to dislike you if you start making a nuisance of yourself. If you let him know how you feel about him, you will probably embarrass him, and then he really will avoid you. I'm not telling you to stop feeling the way you do. It wouldn't do any good if I did. I am telling you to try to keep your feelings to yourself."

She came over and put an arm around me. I was still sort of sniffling. "Why don't you switch some of the emotional energy you're spending on Dwight to doing something for yourself?"

"Like what?"

"Well, like becoming this good horsewoman your father is so anxious for. And how about this book you said you were at work on? Or learning how to cook? I can think of a dozen things that would be more of a help toward growing up than being in a tizzy all the time over Dwight."

"I'm never going to stop feeling the way I do about Dwight."

"Maybe not," said Mom, "but most evidence is

against you. Now run upstairs and wash your face. I see your Dad and the visitor headed this way."

I hugged her back and went upstairs.

We drove to Woodside in Missy's little red car. She had insisted on bringing the lunch, but Mom fixed up a box of cookies and added some beer for Dad.

As we were about to start, Missy handed her car keys to Dad. "I've been driving for more years than you've been born. But I know you'll enjoy the trip more if you're at the wheel," she said.

She offered the front seat to Mom, but Mom wouldn't take it.

"Melinda and I will be fine back here."

I was grateful to Mom for this arrangement. The last thing on earth I wanted was to be marooned with this meddling old stranger, trying to make conversation with her. I have to admit, though, that I liked her a little bit better for letting Dad drive.

Woodside is roughly a hundred miles from our house, so Dad and Mom had plenty of chance to get acquainted with Missy before we got there. Missy asked a lot of questions about their work, and she tried to talk to me about Ethan. She sat squirmed around in her bucket seat as she talked to Mom and me in the back. I was sitting right behind her, so she couldn't see me as well as she could Mom. Which was a good thing. I still hadn't gotten over my disappointment at having to leave Dwight all by himself. I answered mostly "Yes" and "No" and let Missy think I was shy. I knew Mom wanted to shake me, and the back of Dad's neck looked stiff. I could tell they were ashamed of the way I was acting and, to be honest, I couldn't blame them.

Gradually I found myself listening to Missy. She is a good talker, and because she has lived so long she has had a lot of things happen to her, good and bad. Once she told about a dumb thing she had done and it was so funny I just had to laugh along with Dad and Mom. I thought sure now she would look around at me to let me know how happy she was that I was joining the human race, like most grown-ups would have. But Missy just kept looking ahead and ignored me the rest of the way to Woodside. By the time we got there I wasn't feeling sullen any more.

The show was being held on the grounds of the San Mateo Sheriff's Mounted Patrol. It was well outside the town in a heavily wooded area. When we arrived, a fairly large number of horse trailers were parked off to one side. There was a large clubhouse with a terrace outside from which one could see both riding rings. I learned later that one ring was for Western riding and one for English. There were no stables, so the horses were either tied to their trailers or were being walked around under the trees by their owners.

"Oh, isn't this marvelous?" cried Missy, giving Mom's arm a squeeze. "Look at all those Morgans! Do you suppose one of them is meant for me?"

"I doubt it," Dad told her. "These are show horses and probably not for sale. Certainly not for lease. But there may be something back at their barns you could get."

It was almost noon. Dad carried our lunch things up to the terrace and found a table for them. While Mom and Missy unpacked and spread out the food, Dad went out to mingle with the crowd, and I went with him. After all, this was my very first horse show, and as long as I was here, I might as well learn as much as I could. Sooner or later I would have to be taking part in one.

There were already horses at the rings. The classes had started as early as 8:30 this morning.

Dad wanted to get here earlier, but Mom had begged off. "A half a day of it will do me very nicely," she had said. Missy had felt the same way. For my part, as long as I couldn't stay home, I didn't care one way or another. But now, here on the grounds, I began to feel a little interest in what was going on.

"There's Mrs. Towers," Dad said, sounding pleased and starting off at once toward a very large trailer fastened to a truck with a camper top. Both vehicles were painted the same color and were very smart looking. "Morgan Manor" was painted in big letters all over both of them. More or less.

"Hi," called Mrs. Towers as we came up to them. They shook hands and then Mrs. Towers introduced Dad to her husband. "I don't believe I remember your name," she said to me.

"Melinda," said Dad, and Mr. Towers shook hands warmly with me.

"Mr. Ross bought that Granite Ranch stallion," she explained to Mr. Towers.

The three grown-ups chatted for a minute, and I was just stood there feeling dumb when all at once I remembered something.

"Did you bring the little foal?" I asked.

"That we did," said Mrs. Towers. "Want to see him?"

She took me to the end of the trailer and opened its tailgate. "There he is with his mama."

He had grown since I had seen him, but he was still the same adorable little thing, and I wished again that Dad had bought him for me.

"We're going to show him in the dam and produce class," Mrs. Towers informed me.

We went back to where Dad and Mr. Towers stood talking.

"Jane, Mr. Ross has a friend with him today who is looking for a gelding to lease. Know anybody who has one?"

Mrs. Towers thought a minute. "I'm not sure about a gelding, but I think Isabel Jones might be willing to lease her old show mare. She's here today with a couple of horses. You might talk to her."

"Where will I find her?" asked Dad.

Mrs. Towers shrugged and looked vaguely around. "She might be anywhere. That's her trailer over there." She pointed and I saw a two-horse trailer with "Pacheco Morgans" printed on its side.

"Wasn't she entered in the pleasure driving, novice, mares?" Mr. Towers asked.

"Right," his wife answered. "She's in the ring right now."

They quickly got out their program and skimmed it. "She's number 69," said Mrs. Towers.

"Thanks a lot," said Dad. "Come on, Melinda. Let's go watch the pleasure driving class."

"Novice, mares," I added.

Dad chuckled and gave my pigtail a gentle pull. "You're getting the range already, kid. Do you know what 'novice' means?"

Of course I didn't and said so.

"It's a horse that hasn't won more than two blue ribbons. 'Maiden' is a class for horses that have won no blue ribbons."

I laughed for the second time that day. "It's funny to think of a gelding or a stallion being a maiden."

Dad didn't answer. We were approaching the ring, and I doubt that he even heard me.

Number 69 was a middle-aged woman with dark hair set in a kind of bouffant style. She had a lap robe over her knees and was riding in a light, elegant-looking two-wheeled cart. Her horse's harness was highly polished, as was her horse. She held a rein in each hand, high up above her lap. "Road trot, please," sounded from the loudspeaker. "Road trot."

As if on signal, although I couldn't see that she did a blessed thing, her horse lengthened its stride. It was as if it understood the announcement. She whizzed past two other carts like the one she was in and fell in behind a small four-wheel buggy. Around the ring they went, now at a walk, now at a pleasure trot, until the order came for them to line up in the middle of the ring. Helpers ran into the ring to wipe off the horses' noses and necks and to straighten harness. Then they took up their places in front of their own particular horse and tried to get its attention as the judge came up to them. They waved cloths, even stopped to throw up handfuls of dirt in an effort to make the horse look sharp. When the judging was over, number 69 had won second place.

We watched her drive out of the ring, and then we went up to the terrace where Mom and Missy were waiting for us.

"My goodness, but it does take me back to watch those Morgans in harness," said Missy. "I used to drive when I was young. Not much older than you, Melinda." She turned to me. "And it wasn't for show. I ran errands with Old Bess. But if I'd held my reins up under my nose like that, I'd have been laughed off the ranch."

"Where did you grow up, Miss Zinn?" asked Mom, starting to serve up the lunch.

"In Sonoma County, in the Valley of the Moon."

"Jack London's country," said Dad.

"Yes, my father knew him."

"Who was Jack London?" I asked.

Missy looked shocked. "Haven't you ever read *The Call of the Wild*?"

I shook my head.

"What's the world coming to?" asked Missy under her breath.

But I thought it might hang together even if I had never heard of Jack London or *The Call of the Wild*.

I had to admit it was a good lunch even if a meddling old woman had prepared it. Missy fried the chicken in the oven the way Mom does, and she had added a lot of drumsticks. She had made bread and butter sandwiches and a salad that was out of this world. It had everything I like in it, including shrimp. The dressing was outstanding, and Mom asked her for the recipe. Right then and there Missy whisked a notepad and a pencil out of her purse and wrote down the recipe. She was sitting beside me and I could read what she was putting down. To my surprise, buttermilk was one of the things that went into the dressing. Buttermilk! I hate buttermilk; I never touch it. But I had really thought that dressing was neat, and I hoped Mom would make it often.

This got me to thinking. Maybe if enough of the things you like were mixed up with the things you didn't like, then maybe you could end up liking those things. Or not really disliking them. That sounds sort of confused, but you know what I mean. Take this horse business. I have never liked horses. But I like Ethan. And not only because he is the reason Dwight has been at our place so much lately. I like Ethan because he is beautiful and because he is gentle and intelligent. At least, intelligent for a horse. Dad says they have very small brains for their size. Not unlike the dinosaurs of old. I had enjoyed cleaning the barn and I was having a good time at this show. I still wasn't glad I had come, but now that I was here, it was okay. And I really loved that little foal. So what with one thing and another, I might in time begin liking horses as horses. I might even like riding them.

When lunchtime was over and the announcer was calling for the first class of the afternoon, Missy started out to find Isabel Jones.

"Come with me, Mr. Ross. You'll know better how to talk to her. We can all go," she said, looking toward Mom.

"If it's all the same to you, I'll stay here and watch the rings. Good luck."

"Thanks," said Missy. She turned to me. "You'd better come with us, Melinda, because if things work out the way I hope, you're going to be involved in my arrangement with Isabel Jones."

I looked at Dad, and he looked as puzzled as I felt. How on earth could I become involved in Miss Zinn's getting a horse? But neither of us said anything and she didn't explain.

We found Mr. and Mrs. Jones at their trailer. We introduced ourselves all around and Missy took a moment to describe the beautiful Morgan gelding I own.

"Lucky girl!" said Mrs. Jones, and I tried my best to look lucky. Along with a lot of other things, horses were turning me into a first-class hypocrite.

"Lease my old mare?" Mrs. Jones thought for a moment. "I've never leased a horse before. Do you know about this mare?" Missy shook her head. "She's a grand champion park mare. When we retired her from the ring five years ago, we thought of course that we'd breed her. But she's barren. Totally barren. We've tried everything, and nothing works."

"What's wrong with her?" asked Dad.

"You tell me," said Mrs. Jones. "There doesn't seem to be anything wrong with her. Six vets have examined her, and they all declare she's normal."

"She's not normal," said Dad. "That's for sure."

Mr. Jones shrugged. "Normal or not, the result's the same. She can't be got in foal."

"I had thought I wanted a gelding," said Missy, "but the idea of riding a grand champion appeals to me. She must be a beautiful Morgan."

"She was, but we haven't done anything with her for a long time. She's twelve years old now," Mrs. Jones said. She looked at Dad. "What do you think would be a fair price for leasing her?"

Dad thought a minute. "How about fifty dollars a month? Does that sound reasonable?"

"Yes, it does to me. How about you, John?" She had turned to her husband.

"Suits me. The horses are your show. I just build houses."

96

"That seems very fair," said Missy. "When may I see her?"

"Anytime," said Mrs. Jones. "Our ranch, Pacheco Morgans, is just west of Los Banos in the San Joaquin Valley." She went over to her pickup and reached into its glove compartment. "Here's our card," she said. "With thirty Morgans, I'm almost always home."

Missy took the card. "I'd like to come as soon as possible." She looked at Dad. "Would next Sunday suit you? I'd like you to go with me if you can. You know so much more about all this than I do."

"I'll have to check with Lynn," he told her. To the Joneses, he said, "I look forward to seeing your Morgans."

Another weekend shot. But this time I didn't feel anything special. Easter vacation was coming up, when Dwight would be working on the ring every day.

"By the way," said Missy as we started to leave, "what is the name of this mare?"

"Merry Jo," Mrs. Jones told her. "Oakhill's Merry Jo."

"Pretty," said Missy. We said our good-byes and returned to Mom.

For the next two hours I watched Morgans walk

97

and trot and canter. I saw riders posting, jumping, and cantering. It reached the point where all the horses began to look alike, and the riders, too.

It was Missy who ended it. "Melinda," she said, "you have been a very patient girl. I think it's time we took you home."

I slept most of the way.

7

Oakhill's Merry Jo

I've been so busy describing the events leading up to Ethan and Missy that I haven't taken time to go into some matters that maybe I should have before now. Like how I have gone about writing this book.

To begin with, I haven't made a secret of the fact that I *am* writing a book. Except I haven't told Diana. She might not make fun of me. But then again she might, and I don't want to take that chance. You already know that I have discussed it with Missy.

What I do is I go up to my room and work on it there. I work on it in the afternoons after I have done my homework. And sometimes I work on it in the evenings if there's nothing I want to watch on TV. Or there's something on that my parents don't want me to watch. Which happens.

Dad said one evening, "It seems to me you have an awful lot of homework these days."

"It's not all homework," I told him. "I'm writing a book."

"Good for you," he said, and he didn't smile at all. "What's it about?"

"It's about my becoming a horsewoman," I said. "You're in it and Ethan and Missy and Mom. It's about a lot of things."

He looked very seriously at me. "I hope you'll let me read it when it's finished."

"I'll see," I said.

I didn't want to promise I would, because right away I would feel I had someone looking over my shoulder every time I sat down to write. I knew, also, that he would never try to read it on the sly. Neither would my mom. They want to know what I am doing, but they respect my privacy. That's very important, I think.

Our house is very old-fashioned. Not a bit like Diana's. For one thing, it has only one bathroom.

It's upstairs with the three bedrooms. Mom says a nice bathroom could be made out of the big walk-in closet in her and Dad's bedroom. Their bedroom is good-sized, but mine is small, as is the third one. The last two are tucked up under the roof, with dormer windows. My room is real cozy, especially when it rains. You can hear the drops coming down right over your head. You can't hear the rain on the roof at Diana's house.

Dad made me some bookshelves out of bricks and boards. They hold my schoolbooks, and now, of course, the books that Missy brings to me and that I take home from the school library. I hardly read at all before I knew Missy, but now I read at least a book a week, and they are not all skinny ones, either. We are not a bookish family. But Missy has managed to get me charged up about reading, and while reading a book is not as easy as watching TV, you can do it whenever you want to. And it's nice to have a good book around when there's nothing on TV you want to watch. Then, of course, I have taken seriously what Missy said about reading and writing going together. Because I have decided I want to be a writer. I like sitting up here at my little table with my notebook in front of me and a mug of sharpened pencils at one side, like Missy has, and putting my thoughts in the notebook. It's really fun, and if you've never tried it, you should. I use my allowance money to buy the notebooks and pencils. Missy gave me the pencil sharpener.

So now you know how I am writing this book.

The Sunday we went to look at Merry Jo was Palm Sunday, just one week before Easter vacation, during which time Dwight would be working on the riding ring, as I said earlier.

The ring was shaping up, but there was still a lot to do on it. The postholes were all dug, and some of the fencing up. The bulldozer had been in to level the whole thing, and trucks had dumped sand the length of it. But there was still a lot for Dwight and Dad to do. It had rained some days, so they couldn't work. But the rains were welcome when they did come, because they didn't come nearly often enough. We were actually having a drought.

We were to pick Missy up after church. Dad said there was no point in her driving all the way up the valley to our house when we had to go back to Highway One anyway.

Missy lives in the Highlands on a cliff overlooking the Pacific Ocean. She had her house built for her years ago, and it's not like any other house in the world, I'll bet. It's not like an old lady's house at all. There's this huge living room and an enormous granite fireplace. The kitchen is off the entrance hall and has a wide opening over the sink into the living room. Upstairs is a loft bedroom and bath. Her study is off the living room. Behind it is a bedroom and bath. And that's all. The living room ceiling is beamed and high to make room for the loft bedroom. But you can hear the rain on it. And you can hear the ocean crashing on the rocks below the windows. There are bookshelves everywhere, full of books. I think it's a neat house and so does Dad. But Mom says she prefers a kitchen separate from the living room and would miss not having a dining room. She does admit that the house seems just right for Missy, though.

We went again in Missy's little red car, and Dad drove. First she shut Fancy, her whippet, in the garage. There is a side door from the garage into the back patio, so Fancy can come and go. Missy almost always leaves her there when she goes out for any length of time. Of course, with the four of us, there would be no room in the car for Fancy.

This time we didn't take a lunch because Missy

had invited us to have Sunday dinner with her at a nice restaurant in San Juan Bautista, a little town just off the freeway leading to Pacheco Pass. The pass cuts through the hills into the San Joaquin Valley.

Pacheco Pass is beautiful in the spring. Even in this dry spring the hills were still green and the oaks that dot them were putting out their new, bright leaves. As we wound our way between the hills, we could see Pacheco Creek below us with the old sycamores lining its banks. There was only a trickle of water in it, though. And when we came to the San Luis Reservoir, the lake was very, very low. A drought is a dreadful thing. What can live without water? And the rainy season was almost over. It would be hard on the crops and would increase the chance of forest fires.

We found Pacheco Morgans without any trouble. Mr. and Mrs. Jones had put Merry Jo into their riding ring, and we went straight through their big barn to the ring out back. There she stood looking at us, and she was pretty. Of course, she had been out in pasture for a long time (for the past year, Mrs. Jones said), so her coat wasn't what it would have been if she had been groomed every day. It was a very dark brown, what they call liver chestnut, and she had a long star on her face. Her ears were small and her eyes were large. She was smaller than Ethan, more delicate looking. Dad said her head was more refined than Ethan's. Her cannon bones were light and her feet small. Altogether an elegant and very typey Morgan.

"I like her," said Missy, after she had studied the mare for a minute.

"You want to try her out, of course," said Mrs. Jones.

Missy shook her head. "No, I'll have to break into riding very gradually. But I'd be glad if you'd ride her, Cal," she said, turning to Dad.

Of course, this was just what he wanted. So Mr. Jones went into the ring, took hold of Merry Jo's halter, and led her into the barn. In no time she was saddled and bridled and Dad was mounting her in the ring.

This was the first time I had really seen my father on a horse. He had been working Ethan, of course, first in the long lines and then under a saddle, and he was going well. But now Dad was on a fully trained horse, a grand champion park horse. Something he could really ride. He circled the ring once at a walk, then he moved Merry Jo into a trot. She went very collected. That is, her nose was tucked under and her neck arched. She looked really neat, and she was lifting her feet high. Dad was wearing the happiest grin I'd seen on his face for a long time. He slowed her to a walk, then signaled her to canter. She took off like a dream and went around and around the ring like a rocking horse, never changing speed. He reversed her, and she went as well.

My dad is good at a lot of things. He can fix a leaky faucet and carve a real neat Halloween pumpkin. He always gets the lights just right on the Christmas tree and does ever so many useful things. As fathers go, you couldn't want a better one. Except, of course, for this horse thing.

But not until this day at Pacheco Morgans have I ever felt that I wanted to shout, "Hey, that's my dad!" The way he was riding that mare was something special. It made your blood tingle to watch him. You could see he was loving every minute. And so was Merry Jo. She couldn't have lifted her feet higher if there had been a judge in the ring.

Missy spoke at my side. "Do you suppose we'll ever be able to ride like that?"

"Nope," I said promptly. "I bet there aren't many people in the world who can ride like that."

"I think you're right, Melinda," she said.

At last he rode up to the gate where all of us stood watching.

"She's great," he said, "just great. But she's a lot of horse. I wonder if she might be too much for you," he added, looking at Missy.

"We'll never know until we try," she answered him. "After all, I'm only leasing her, and if she doesn't work out, we can bring her back."

Dad nodded.

Mrs. Jones spoke. "One thing, she has no bad habits. Doesn't kick, bite, or buck. And she's good on the trail. My girls ride her all over the countryside. She isn't afraid of a thing."

"That's important," said Dad. "More important than anything else."

Missy told Mrs. Jones she had arranged with Dodge Rayburn to pick up Merry Jo with his truck and trailer the following Wednesday if she decided she wanted her.

"We'll be here sometime around midday."

"Are you going to board her with Dodge Rayburn?" Mrs. Jones asked.

"I haven't decided yet," Missy answered.

Dad spoke. "Missy, you can't possibly take the mare away unless you are sure you know where you're going to put her."

That funny light came into Missy's eyes. "Dodge is saving a stall for me, just in case."

"Just in case of what?" Dad wanted to know.

"We'll talk about it later, Cal. If you don't mind."

Right away I began to get suspicious. Ever since Woodside I had been thinking off and on about what Missy had said about me having something to do with Merry Jo. She hadn't given Dad a straight answer, and I was sure the reason had something to do with what she had said at Woodside. But I couldn't figure out what it was.

Before we left Pacheco Morgans, Mrs. Jones asked us into the house for coffee and cake. There was a lot of horse talk about breeding lines, training, and such. But I didn't really listen. I was still trying to puzzle out what was on Missy's mind. The cake was just about as good as Mom's, and I had two pieces.

Missy and Mom did most of the talking on the way back to San Juan Bautista. Dad was unusually quiet, and I knew he was worried about what Missy had in mind to do about Merry Jo.

It all came out as soon as we were seated in the restaurant. We had given our orders and were looking silently out the window by our table at the view of the Salinas valley stretching below us and to the east, the Gavilans towering into the dusky sky. Then Missy spoke, breaking the silence.

"Now, I want to tell you what I have in mind for Merry Jo."

Every Ross eye was on her.

"I want to board her at your stable, Cal."

Astonished silence followed her announcement.

"It makes perfect sense," she hurried on. "I'll be taking lessons from you two or three times a week, and my horse will be where my teacher is. Much more convenient for you." She turned to look at me. "It seems that you'll have two horses to feed every morning instead of one, Melinda. Shall you object to that?"

I didn't know what to say and just stared across at Dad. Mom was obviously waiting for him to speak. He opened his mouth, but Missy spoke before he could get a word out.

"I will pay you the same amount for board as Dodge charges, which is one hundred dollars a month."

"I wouldn't charge you that much, Missy. Dodge

is in the business of boarding horses. I'm not."

"One hundred dollars or nothing," declared Missy. "Some places are charging more than that. Please say you'll take her, Cal. It will make it so much nicer for both of us."

He looked around at Mom.

"It's up to you, Cal," she told him. "I think Melinda should be considered, though."

I felt their eyes on me as I fidgeted with my knife and fork.

"Well, Melinda?" Dad asked.

I looked up at him. "It's okay with me."

"All right," said Dad. "At least we can give it a try. We'll have to keep Ethan and the mare separated for a while, but that should be no problem. One can stay in the paddock and one in the barn, change and change about. When the ring is finished, they can both be outside." He turned again to Mom. "What do you say we double Melinda's allowance now that she will be responsible in the morning for two horses instead of one?"

"I think that's very fair," said Mom. "But I don't believe she should spend six dollars a week. Some of it must be saved."

"How much?" I asked.

"Three dollars of it," said Mom.

110

"But that's my whole raise," I cried, just as the waitress appeared with the first course.

"Correct," agreed Mom calmly, picking up her salad fork.

It was a good salad. Blue cheese dressing.

The next week was fun. Diana and I spent every day together. Mom had arranged with Diana's mother to let me stay at their house. Since it was Easter vacation and my mom was away at her job all day, I couldn't stay alone until Dad came home. But fortunately Dwight was working at our place, and my mom said it was okay for us two to stay there as long as he was there. When he rode down the hill to his house for lunch on his ten-speed bike, we had to follow him. Every morning Mom would put up a bag lunch for Diana and for me. The lunches were always the same for both of us, but we never knew what was in them. So eating was a kind of adventure.

One day Missy took us both to lunch at The Wharf in Monterey. The restaurant is famous for its fish dinners and is quite expensive. So you can't blame Missy for being disgusted when we both ordered meatballs and spaghetti.

On Wednesday of that week, not long after Dad

got home, Dodge Rayburn and Missy drove in with Merry Jo. Dad had already turned Ethan out into the paddock and closed the paddock barn door on him. There was hay in Merry Jo's manger and a good bed of shavings on the floor.

Dad walked her around for a while after she was unloaded to rest her after her long ride. She hesitated about going into the barn, but Dad was patient with her and at last she went in.

Then Missy and Dodge Rayburn drove down to the red barn where Missy had left her car when they started for Pacheco Morgans.

Now there were two horses at the Ross barn, and Dad had a hundred dollars a month to apply against the expense of keeping Ethan. With riding lesson fees to boot.

That night at dinner he said, "As soon as you have time, Lynn, I wish you'd take Melinda and get her outfitted with a riding habit."

"Will do," said Mom.

Suddenly my appetite was gone—and we were having tripe Spanish, my very favorite dish. Ordinarily I would have been thrilled at the prospect of a lot of new clothes. But a riding habit! I could hear horses pounding through the dining room, and my heart was pounding with them. The whole ghastly business of riding was coming closer and closer. And there was no way I could avoid it now, even if I wanted to. With a horse in the barn and a riding habit in my clothes closet, I was stuck.

8

Boots and Saddles

On the very next Saturday after that tripe Spanish dinner, Mom took me to a store right here in the valley that caters to horse people. It has everything you want for a horse except, maybe, shoes. Saddles, bridles, blankets—you name it, they've got it. And the clothes to go with them.

In spite of the fact that I dreaded having a riding habit in my closet, I had to admit to myself as soon as I began looking at them that I liked the clothes you ride in.

Dad had dictated my riding habit. It seems you wear different outfits for different kinds of riding. Since I was to be a saddle seat, equitation rider,

I wouldn't be wearing high boots with breeches tucked in. Instead I was to have something called jodhpurs, a fairly tight-fitting pair of pants that flare at the ankle and cover the instep of your boot. Jodhpur boots come just above the ankle. You're not supposed to wear a hard hat with this outfit, but Dad said for the sake of safety I was to wear a hard hat at all times.

I picked out a pair of dark blue jodhpurs with a blouse and belt to match and a pair of black jodhpur boots. We got a plastic hard hat. They are less expensive than the velvet ones and are just as protective. Mine was bright red and looked really neat.

If I do say so, that riding habit made me look terrific. Riding clothes make anyone who isn't fat look better. There I stood grinning at myself in the full-length mirror. Suddenly, on an impulse, I gathered up my braid and tucked it inside my hard hat. You wouldn't believe what it did for me. I easily looked four years older. Anyway, three.

I couldn't wait to get home and show it all to Dad and Dwight. I knew they were hanging the gate on the ring this morning. It was all finished except the gate. After today Ethan and Merry Jo could both be outside all day. One in the paddock and one in the ring.

We hadn't laid eyes on Missy since she had delivered Merry Jo to our place. She had phoned a couple of times to make sure all was well with her horse. She explained that she wouldn't be seeing us until after Easter since her brother and his wife were coming up from San Diego to spend Easter with her. Above all things, she didn't want them to know about Merry Jo.

"He'll have a conniption fit if he knows I'm planning to ride," she told Dad on the phone.

Dad was laughing when he hung up. "She said her brother is always warning her to watch her step. But Missy said that when you're old enough to have to watch your step, you aren't going anywhere."

When we got home with all my purchases, I ran upstairs to my room. The first thing I did was put my hair up. I found some bobby pins in the bathroom. I fixed it sort of low on my neck like some of the girls I had seen at Woodside. Then I got into my new outfit and went out to the ring.

Dad saw me first. Dwight had his back to me. Dad let out a "Wow! Look who's here!" At that, Dwight turned around. For just a split second he didn't know who I was. Then he smiled a slow smile. "You look like the real thing," he said, and turned back to his work. It wasn't much of a compliment, but for a tiny instant he had looked at me with real interest.

Dad looked me over carefully. "You look really great, Melinda. Now let's see what that outfit will look like on a horse."

I gasped. "Not Ethan; he's got another month to go."

"He'll be okay," said Dad, starting toward the barn. "I'll have him on a longe line."

This was the last thing I had expected. And vanity had got me into it. How I wished I had put my riding clothes safely away in my closet where I could forget them for another month! Now I was stuck. And all because I had to show Dwight how much older I looked in riding clothes and with my hair up. I wanted to kick myself.

In no time at all Dad had Ethan saddled. Instead of his bridle he was wearing his halter with what looked like yards of rather narrow white canvas attached to it. Dad explained that this was a longe line (pronounced as if it were spelled l-u-n-g-e). He led Ethan over to the mounting block, which was just like the one at Dodge Rayburn's, an old stump. I got up on it, Dad held Ethan's head, and, remembering what I had done at the red barn, I swung up into the saddle. Of course, I was terrified. Out of the tail of my eye I could see that Dwight was watching. That put a little courage into me.

Dad led Ethan over to the ring, Dwight held the gate open, and we went inside. Unlike my first ride on Sam, this time I didn't even have any reins. Besides that, this time I was riding on a flat, cut-back saddle with no space between it and Ethan's withers. What would I hang onto if something happened?

As if reading my thoughts, Dad said, "If you need to grab something, grab hold of his mane."

"I feel more secure with reins," I told him. "I promise not to pull."

He shook his head. "I don't want you to have reins until you get your balance. That way you won't spoil Ethan's mouth by using them as handles to hang onto. Some riders think reins are a kind of lifeline. They aren't."

From beside Ethan's head he studied me for a moment as I sat motionless in the saddle. "Keep your thighs pressed into him and your heels down. And try to relax."

We started along the rail. Ethan stepped more quickly and lightly than Sam, but he was going quietly and steadily. Round and round the ring we went. I had raised my eyes from his ears and was beginning to relax.

"Put your hands out in front of you, thumbs on top, as if you were holding the reins, and keep looking ahead of you and not at Ethan's ears," Dad commanded.

I did as he said and felt awfully foolish with my hands stuck out in front of me and no reins in them.

"Elbows at the sides," ordered Dad, and I pressed in with my elbows. "Not so tight," he said, "just easy."

Round and round the ring we went and, very gradually, I began looking around me, at the hills rising up across the road, at Dwight busy at the gate, off toward the barn where Merry Jo stood lazily in the sunshine. Then down at Dad leading Ethan.

He grinned up at me. "You are completely relaxed."

I nodded.

"Now take your feet out of the stirrups."

I did and let them hang down as we did another circle of the ring. Dad must have walked a couple of miles by this time. A more patient—or determined—man you couldn't even imagine.

At last he stopped Ethan.

"Now put your right leg over the front of the saddle and sit sideways on it."

I did, and there I sat facing him.

"Now put your right leg over the back of the saddle and turn yourself toward Ethan's head."

I did as he told me.

"Now you have turned yourself all the way around in the saddle. And Ethan stood perfectly still and let you do it. Doesn't that give you a little more confidence in him and yourself?"

I nodded, but I was feeling pretty shaky inside.

Dad then went to the center of the ring and let out a good stretch of longe line.

"I'm going to start him in a small circle, Melinda. First at a walk, then at a very slow trot."

"Dad, I'm scared."

He walked up to me, gathering up the longe line as he came. He laid a hand on my thigh.

"You have a good seat and you have nothing to be afraid of. I can promise you that Ethan won't buck or do anything foolish. I've been riding him for a month now, and he's hardly taken a wrong step. He wants to do what you want him to do. He's that kind of horse. I never trained an easier one. So now let's try a walk first and then a slow trot."

I looked down into Dad's eyes. They were looking pleadingly into mine. Suddenly I thought of Martin and all Dad had lost in losing him.

"Okay," I said.

Dad spoke to Ethan, and he moved forward at a good brisk walk. Then before I knew it, he began to trot. It was a slow trot, not much faster than his walk. But it was a trot all right, and I could feel the difference. I was bumping up and down, and it couldn't have been very comfortable for poor Ethan's back. We made two circles, then Dad pulled him down to a walk.

"Now, was that so bad?" he demanded.

I shook my head.

"Okay, let's try it again. This time don't worry about sitting up straight. Try to keep your heels down, but think of yourself as a sack of potatoes and slump down in the saddle. That way your back will relax and you won't bump so much."

We tried it again and it did actually go better this time. Once I grabbed hold of the front of Ethan's mane and Dad never said a word. He was letting me find the best way I could to feel safe. This gave me more confidence.

At last he said, "Now you can dismount."

He went to Ethan's head and I tried to remember what I had done when I got off Sam. For a minute I just sat there while Dad smiled up at me. Then it all came back. I swung my right foot out of the stirrup and over Ethan's rump, leaned into the saddle, and slid to the ground. It was easy.

"Good," said Dad. "Now I want you to mount him."

I looked off toward the mounting block.

"No," said Dad, "this time I want you to mount him from the ground."

He told me exactly how to do it. It didn't sound complicated. The hard part was getting my left foot up into the stirrup. But I finally did. I gave a couple of little hops on one foot while my left hand gripped a handful of mane and my right hand was on the cantle, or back, of the saddle. Then up I heaved myself and there I was, looking between Ethan's ears.

"Good work!" said Dad, grinning joyously. "Now let's try it again."

I did it three times before he called it quits. Then

we led Ethan out of the ring. As we passed through the gate where Dwight was setting the last screws to its hinges, I heard him say almost under his breath, "Nice going."

He never looked up from his work as he said it, but I felt *almost* as if I could go back and do the whole thing over just to hear him say those words again.

That evening Diana phoned me. She always calls after dinner when Mom and I have cleaned up the kitchen. There is no telephone privacy in our house. The phone is in the kitchen and whoever is in there can hear every word you say.

What Diana had to say was as startling as the two words Dwight had spoken at the gate.

"Guess what?" she began.

"What?" I dutifully asked.

"At dinner tonight Dwight said you were a kookie kid but you had a lot of guts."

I just managed to say, "Thanks, Diana," before I hung up. Then I went straight to my room to think and think about today, when I had had my first ride on Ethan and Dwight had paid me three compliments. Three! And Diana had been nice enough to tell me. I decided to call her back in a few minutes.

But right now I just wanted to think.

The next day was Easter Sunday. The church was full of flowers and smelled wonderful. The service was much longer than usual, but Father John was having such a good time no one minded. The church was crowded, for this is the big day for Christians, bigger even than Christmas. Mom had bought me a new dress, yellow with little sprigs of green flowers all over it. She said it went well with my green eyes and blond hair. I wore a new yellow sweater with it, and I felt as if I looked nice. Mom and Dad looked nice, too. They were wearing their very best clothes, though they weren't new. After church Dad took us into Carmel for brunch. Then we walked around the town in the spring sunshine, feeling happy about everything.

Next day was school again. And the day after that, when Dad and I drove home in the afternoon, there was Missy. She was wearing riding breeches and high, black, shiny boots, a riding jacket, and a black velvet hard hat.

"Missy, you look smashing!" Dad greeted her.

"Do I really?" she asked, her eyes shining with that special glow. "I've been dying to get into them, but my brother and his wife didn't leave until rather late yesterday. They were going to spend the night with friends in Santa Barbara. So I had to wait until today. I took a chance that you'd be able to give me my first lesson today, Cal. Can you?"

"That I can," said Dad. He turned to me. "Run and put on your jodhpurs, honey. I'll give you both a lesson."

So it had begun. From now on I could expect to ride Ethan several times a week and probably twice on Saturday. Of course, I wasn't handling him yet. Dad would do all the saddling and bridling—when I got around to a bridle—and he would be in the ring with me at all times. But my equitation training had begun.

Missy opened the turtle of her little red car and it was full of riding gear. A new Argentine jump-seat saddle, a new saddle pad, and a new bridle. Dad had told her what to get and she had gotten it. He held up the bridle.

"It looks okay if the bit isn't too wide. Let's try it on her."

We all went into the barn. Merry Jo had been in the ring, but Missy had caught her up and taken her to the barn for grooming and saddling. Dad haltered her and led her out of her stall and cross-tied her. Then he started working with the bridle. When he had it about right, he slipped off her halter and put the bridle on. It was a perfectly plain bridle with a single rein and snaffle bit. He shortened some more straps and at last pronounced it just right. Then he saddled her up, and she was ready for Missy and the ring.

I hadn't gone in to change yet because I was interested in how all the new tack would fit Merry Jo. And now I hung around because I wanted to see how this old lady would act when she took her first ride in an English saddle. Even if it wasn't a flat saddle, like mine, it was still a whole lot flatter than any Western saddle ever could be. And she had ridden only Western before now.

I might have known it. Missy never turned a hair. She led that little mare over to the mounting block, gathered her reins in her left hand, seized some mane, grabbed the cantle of the saddle, and swung up as if she had been doing it all her life.

"Are you sure you need me, Missy?" Dad asked.

She laughed. "Getting on a horse is like riding a bicycle. Once you've learned, you never forget how to do it. But I don't know how to post, and I know my canter will be very ragged. Yes, I need help all right, Cal."

She walked Merry Jo toward the ring, and Dad opened the gate for her. Actually it is constructed so you can open it from a horse's back.

"I'm just going to walk her around for a while," said Missy. "It's been thirty years since I was on a horse and I have to get the feel of it again."

"Okay," said Dad, "take your time."

I ran to the house to change into my jodhpurs.

By the time I came out, Dad had moved to the middle of the ring and was instructing Missy. I climbed up onto the fence to watch.

As Missy walked by me for the third time, I heard Dad say, "Now would you like to try a slow trot?"

"Okay," replied Missy.

I saw her shorten her reins, and Merry Jo began to trot. I wouldn't call it very slow. She was very collected and into the bit, and Missy was bumping around a lot. But Missy wasn't hanging onto the reins. Her hands were nice and light, but definitely in contact with the bit. They went halfway around the ring before Dad told her to walk. The minute he said, "Walk," Merry Jo dropped back to a walk. She went on voice command! Missy reached forward to pat her neck.

"You were right, Cal," I heard her say. "She's a lot of horse, but I'm determined to ride her."

While I sat there watching, they took off at another trot. Missy still hadn't found her old sitting trot and bounced a lot. Then at the far end of the ring I saw her come to a full stop. Dad went over to talk to her. I saw her nod her head. The next minute she had Merry Jo into a canter! That old lady was actually cantering and she was riding well. No bouncing now. She needed to improve her sitting trot and she needed to learn to post, but there wasn't a whole lot that Dad would have to teach Missy. Even I could see that.

Merry Jo was into her rocking horse canter, head tucked well under, neck arched, ears pricked. It almost looked as if she were cantering in one spot, though she moved forward. Missy's hands were light on the reins and she was laughing. It was plain to see she was having the time of her life.

All at once I envied her. I, Melinda Ross, ten-years-old-going-on-eleven, was envying an old lady in her seventies. Because Missy wasn't afraid! It hadn't occurred to her since she got on that mare that she would somehow fall off or be thrown off. If only I could be like that!

Why was I so afraid? Perched there on that fence, I tried to figure out what made me so scared of horses. No horse had ever hurt me in my entire life. Ethan even acted as if he liked me, and so did Merry Jo. And I liked them. It made no sense to be afraid of something you liked. But still I *was* afraid.

Missy rode up to where I sat and stopped.

"Oh, Melinda, she's such fun. A really darling horse. I don't know when I've enjoyed myself so much."

"You ride very well, Missy. From what you said, I didn't think you'd ride that well."

"I'm a little surprised myself. But Merry Jo is such a perfect little horse. She makes it easy."

Dad came sauntering up. "Missy, you two complement each other. Merry Jo's just the right size for you. You really look good."

Missy dismounted and threw her reins over the mare's head. "I think I've had enough for the first time out."

Dad nodded. "You may be stiff tomorrow as it is. I wonder how you'd feel about my trying her out on the trail."

"I'd be glad if you would, Cal."

"Okay. I'll give Melinda a lesson and then I'll try her outside the ring. You'll do more trail riding than anything else once you've got used to her."

He went off to the barn to saddle Ethan, and Missy and I were left alone.

I had never discussed my fear of horses with Missy. There had never really been a chance. Come to think of it, this was the first time we had ever been alone together except when she read those first five chapters. While she stood stroking Merry Jo's nose, I thought about confessing to her. I knew she was very old and I thought she was pretty wise. She might know something about horses that even Dad didn't know. So far he hadn't said a thing to me that made me less afraid. He was always telling me I didn't have anything to be afraid of, but he hadn't convinced me. Maybe Missy could.

"Missy, could I ask you a question?"

She looked around Merry Jo's head. "Of course, dear."

"How come you're not afraid to ride? I mean, you're pretty old to be riding. How come you aren't afraid something will happen to you?"

She was perfectly still for about a minute, looking

130

down at her boots, then she raised her eyes to mine.

"Are you afraid?"

I nodded.

"When I was young and starting out, I was afraid. Then I got over it. Just as you will. When you want to do something very much, you just do it. I always loved horses and I wanted to ride more than anything else on earth. So I had to overcome my fear. And I did."

I jumped down off the fence. "But, Missy, *I don't want to ride*. It's my dad that wants me to."

She came around to my side of Merry Jo. "Why on earth does he want you to do something you don't want to do?" She sounded shocked.

"He doesn't understand how afraid I am."

"Then why don't you just tell him you'd rather not? I'm sure he'd see reason if he thought you really hated the whole idea."

"It's not easy to explain." I thought a minute, trying to choose just the right words. "I had a brother, Martin, five years older than I am. He was crazy about horses the way Dad is. Martin died five years ago and I'm all Dad has left. I just have to learn to ride for Martin's sake."

"Oh, Melinda. Oh, you poor, brave child. What

can I say?" She looked frantically toward the barn. "Here comes your father now with Ethan. Just try to remember this. It has always helped me." She looked me hard in the eyes and her own were deeply violet and serious. "The Chinese have an ancient saying: 'That which you fear will come to pass.' If you fear something, you see, it will happen. So don't fear it."

"I'll remember," I whispered as Dad entered the ring leading Ethan on the longe line.

"Your turn, Melinda," he called out.

I walked right over and without a moment's hesitation mounted Ethan smoothly.

Dad turned to Missy. "Would you believe this kid had never mounted a horse from the ground until four days ago?"

"No, I wouldn't," said Missy. "And I'd give anything to be able to get my foot up to a stirrup like that. But I guess it's the mounting block for us old bones."

She went out of the ring with Merry Jo, and my riding lesson began.

That which you fear will come to pass. Then you must stop fearing it if you didn't want it to happen, like Missy said. Dad was walking Ethan in a wide circle.

I leaned forward and patted Ethan's neck. He twitched an ear around at me.

"Good Ethan, good horse," I said to him. "I don't need to be afraid of you, do I?"

His ears twitched again as if in answer, but still I couldn't bring myself to trust him. What if he should jump and I should fall off? But he never *had* jumped. And suppose I did fall off? I wouldn't have far to fall, and the ring was covered with sand almost a foot deep. I had had worse falls in my life and nothing much had happened to me.

All at once I thought to myself, "Okay, so you may fall. So what? It won't kill you or even hurt you much."

I turned my head to look over at Dad. We had been learning about compasses at school. It suddenly occurred to me that the three of us made the two points of a compass, with Dad at the center and Ethan and me the sweeping edge that measured our circle. Dad was looking very serious, his eyes never leaving Ethan and me.

Then a thought hit me with such a shock that I gasped as if cold water had been thrown in my face. I didn't trust my father, either! He had told me over and over again that I had nothing to be afraid of. Yet

I hadn't believed him. I knew I loved him. Love and trust went together. I decided I just had to trust him. Besides, it made sense. I knew my father would never let me ride if I was likely to fall. He would never put me on a horse that would want to throw me. He would never take any chances with me at all.

I looked over at him, and he was smiling at me. I knew, too, why he was smiling. I had been so busy thinking I had forgotten to be afraid! I was all relaxed!

"Let's try a slow trot," he called to me.

"Okay," I called back, and my voice wasn't one bit shaky.

I gave Ethan a touch with my heel, I heard Dad cluck to him, and in seconds we were into a slow trot. To my amazement, I wasn't bumping at all! I was riding, actually riding, for the very first time. I don't know how it happened, but suddenly I had got it all together and I was riding Ethan. He and I were going around and around on the end of that longe line as if we were glued together.

After about ten minutes Dad ended the lesson.

"You're really catching on, Melinda. Tomorrow I'll put the bridle on him. You did very well today."

He put Ethan up and then rode off into the hills on Merry Jo. "I'll only be gone a few minutes," he said.

Missy and I went into the house and sat down in the kitchen.

"You are the bravest person I have ever known, Melinda."

"Oh, Missy, that's ridiculous. Just because I'm trying to ride a horse when I'm afraid."

"Doing something you're afraid to do because you feel you must do it takes great courage. I just hope your father isn't putting too much pressure on you. Does your mother know how you feel?"

I shook my head. "Not anyone knows except Diana, and I don't think it made much impression on her when I told her."

She was silent for a bit. Her eyes were troubled.

"Melinda, I don't want to be a meddler. But would you like to have me speak to your parents about this horse business? I've become very fond of all of you, and it distresses me that you and your Dad are at cross-purposes."

"No, Missy, thanks just the same. I know it means an awful lot to Dad to have me become a good horsewoman. Losing Martin was very hard on him. I feel I want to make it up to him if I can. You see, I really love him."

We were sitting at the little table in the window where we eat our breakfast. She reached over and took my hand.

"You can't live forever in the shadow of your dead brother, dear. It's not your fault that he died, and nothing you can do will bring him back. I am sure your parents wouldn't want you feeling the way you do."

I spoke quickly. "I don't want them ever to know. Promise me you won't ever breathe a word of all this to them, Missy."

"I promise I won't. I just wish there were something I could do to help you."

All at once a thought hit me. "But you have helped me, Missy. You said you wanted to ride more than anything else and so you were able to do it. Well, I don't want to ride, actually. But I want to help my father bear the loss of Martin more than anything else, and the way I can do that is to learn to ride. And so *I'll* be able to do it."

We looked at each other as if we had made a great discovery.

"Good for you, Melinda."

"And that Chinese saying really helps."

Just then Dad came trotting into the yard, and we went out to greet him.

"How did she go?" asked Missy.

"She was perfect. I wouldn't be afraid to see you take her out tomorrow."

"Not tomorrow," returned Missy. "Tomorrow I am planning to spend a lot of time in a hot tub. Day after tomorrow, maybe."

We laughed and waved her off in her little red car. Then Dad and I, with our arms around each other, led Merry Jo to the barn.

9

The Golden West

Nothing much happened in the next two months except that school let out in June. By the time it had, I think you could say that I was well into riding. By that time, too, Ethan had been a gelding for two months, so I could groom him and ride him whenever I wanted to. If I wanted to. *In the ring.* Dad was very firm about my never going out on the trail alone. Never.

I discovered something interesting when I began to take care of Ethan all by myself. After you've picked up a horse's four feet a few times and cleaned out his hoofs, you begin to worry less about him stepping on you. It's as if you had got some control over his feet. While of course this is ridiculous, you certainly do become more familiar with them. The day my darling Ethan held up each of his hind feet in turn for me to clean them, a lot of fear was washed out of me in pure affection for him. And this was the horse that didn't want you to touch his feet in the beginning! How can you go on feeling afraid of anything that tries to be so accommodating?

And another thing. When I began riding Ethan alone, I began to build confidence. I know this sounds funny, because my dad is a good teacher. But a teacher is always reminding you of the things you don't do right. When I was alone with Ethan and put him into a trot and then didn't take off on the proper diagonal, nobody cared. Least of all me. I could concentrate on keeping my posting smooth and in rhythm with my horse. When it began to feel natural and comfortable, then I would check my diagonal and correct it if it needed correction. Most of the time it did.

I'll never forget the day Dad rode Merry Jo into the ring with Ethan and me. (Missy was in New York and had urged Dad to ride her horse whenever he had the time.) We started walking side by side around the ring. Then Dad called for a trot, and I put Ethan into it easily and for once started off on the proper diagonal. This simply means that when your horse puts the foot nearest the rail forward, you rise in the saddle and lower yourself when the foot comes back. It's easy once you get the hang of it.

Today after the trot, which he said was very good, he said, "Now I'll tell you how to put him into a canter." My heart flew into my mouth, so to speak. But I knew better than to argue that I wasn't ready. If Dad said I was, then I was. I thought quickly, "That which you fear will come to pass," made a hasty prayer, and got ready.

"Start him off at a walk, then shorten your reins, give your right rein a little jerk, and at the same time touch him with your right heel. There'll be a slight rise in his forequarters, and then he will settle into the canter smoothly. Now walk."

I did exactly as he told me. Ethan gave a slight jump and then he was cantering. I couldn't believe it! The canter was much easier to ride than the trot! It was almost like a rocking chair. I could feel myself grinning. We went all the way around the ring before Dad said, "Okay, walk." He had been cantering beside me on Merry Jo. Now I looked around at him, a big smile on my face, and before I knew it, he had leaned over and grabbed me around the neck. A hug on horseback. Of course it startled Ethan and he made a little sidestep. Dad let go at once, but it hadn't bothered me a bit.

"That was a fool thing to do, Melinda, but I just couldn't resist it. You were riding the way I hoped someday you would ride. And you looked so darned happy. It's the first time I have seen you look happy on a horse since you got on Sam."

And you know what I did? I laid my face down on Ethan's mane and burst into tears.

"Oh, honey, I'm sorry I scared you." Poor Dad thought I was crying because Ethan had side-stepped.

I straightened up and dashed the tears out of my eyes.

"I wasn't crying because I was scared, Dad. You didn't scare me a bit. I was just crying because I felt so good about everything. You, Ethan, the riding. Everything."

"Well, bless your heart." Then, suddenly, he became all business. "Now, would you like to try another canter? This time on the right lead."

I turned Ethan around, walked him a few steps, then gave a little jerk on the left rein and a touch with my left heel, and away we went on the right lead. At last I had learned to ride. Of course there was still a lot I had to know about equitation, and it would be a long time before I was ready for a show. But, by golly, I could ride. Anyway Ethan.

I must explain about Missy going to New York. She went back to see her publishers. Though Missy is so old, she goes right on writing. Almost a book a year. Her publishers take a great interest in her because her books sell like hotcakes. So every so often they like to have her come back and talk with them about contracts and movie rights (several of Missy's books have been made into movies) and that sort of thing. Missy writes mystery stories. She says it's a mystery to her how she ever came to do that. She started out as a high school English teacher. The first book she ever wrote was about a high school English teacher. It was quite funny and sold pretty well. The next book she wrote didn't sell at all well. And she was about to give up writing when she got this marvelous idea for a mystery story. And she's been writing mysteries ever since. She says right now she is thinking about one that concerns an old lady who buys a fine horse. She says when you're a writer, everything is grist for your mill. Whatever that means.

It's when she told us all this that I began to get the idea for writing this book about a girl who had to learn to be a good horsewoman. But I can't even imagine what my next book will be about. If I ever try to write a next one.

Anyway, that's how Missy happened to be in New York and Dad was riding Merry Jo.

But there have been plenty of times since she got home that for one reason or another she can't get out to ride. Then Dad works Merry Jo for her.

That's what happened one day in June when I was taking my first trail ride. Both horses had been out on the trail, but I never had.

Trail riding, I have discovered, is the nicest kind of riding there is. You're out in the fields or under the trees with shadows on the ground. Everywhere you look, it's beautiful. Anyway, it is here above the Carmel Valley. The horses enjoy it, too. They get bored in the ring. But out on the trail there is a spring in their walk, and they look around with real interest, and their ears go back and forth, catching new sounds.

All at once Dad said, "Get down in the saddle."

This means shorten your reins, push your bottom hard into the saddle, and press in with your thighs.

"There's a deer. Three deer."

"What will Ethan do?" I asked.

"He may try to whirl around, and he may not do anything. But often horses are afraid of deer."

We kept walking on, and all was well until suddenly the horses saw the deer. Both stopped dead in their tracks, and their heads jerked up. Ethan put an arch in his neck and studied the deer. Then after about half a minute he dropped his head to its usual position and walked calmly on! Merry Jo moved quietly beside him.

We both laughed.

"I'd forgotten that Ethan was a range stallion. He's practically lived with deer," Dad said. "And Merry Jo, not being spooky, took her signal from him."

The next morning we saw deer tracks around the old bathtub in the paddock. The drought had dried up the Carmel River, and the poor, thirsty deer were coming to our barn for water. They were welcome to it. From then on I took care to see that the tub was full to the top every evening before I went in to dinner. And every morning a lot of the water had gone and there were deer tracks all around.

The Saturday following that first trail ride, Missy phoned us. She never phones or comes near us on weekends unless there's a Morgan show, when we all go. She says weekends are for families. I answered the phone and she seemed very excited.

"Would it be all right if I came out this morning? I want to talk to your dad about something."

Mom took the phone and told her to come along and stay for lunch. We were having leftover meat loaf sandwiches, and there was enough for everyone. Missy said she'd accept the invitation and be right out.

I hadn't quite finished my Saturday chores when she drove in. Dad had just come in from the barn and was having a mug of coffee.

She came in the back door as usual, and I knew the minute I saw her that something was up. Her eyes were shining. Right away she opened her big shoulder bag and dug into it.

"I've got the prize list for the Golden West," she announced, holding up a thin white pamphlet.

The Golden West is the big championship Morgan horse show that comes to Monterey every year during the first week of July. The prize list names the classes and the awards and rules for each class.

"How about some coffee, Missy?" asked Mom, and Missy thanked her and took the mug Mom filled.

"Is that what you wanted to talk about?" I asked, nodding toward the prize list in her hand.

"Yes, it is," she replied, and her eyes seemed to get brighter than ever.

Dad laughed. "Missy, you're as transparent as cellophane. What have you got on your mind?"

"Just this, Cal. Do you think I'm good enough to ride in the Jack Benny?"

Dad let out a "Wow!" that I'm sure you could hear clear down to Diana's. "You mean it?"

"Of course I mean it, if you think I'm good enough."

Mom sat down by the table in the window with her own mug of coffee. "Forgive my ignorance, but what is the Jack Benny?"

Dad explained. "It's a class for anyone thirty-nine or over. You remember Jack Benny always insisted he was thirty-nine no matter how old he got? You can ride saddle seat or jump seat, on a stallion, a gelding, or a mare. Just about anything goes. Only you have to ride on the proper leads and the proper diagonals. Of course you're good enough, Missy." He shook his head as if he just couldn't believe it. "You and Merry Jo. I can't wait to see that."

From that morning on, Missy was at our place every single day working Merry Jo and putting a fine point on her riding. The show was to start July second, and that very Friday evening was the Jack Benny.

I'll never forget that evening. I was almost as tight inside as if I were going into the ring myself.

Dad and Missy had bathed and polished Merry Jo to the nth degree. They had trimmed her ears and her bridle band, skinned all the whiskers off her nose, and clipped her fetlocks. She looked absolutely beautiful. She shone with such satiny highlights you could almost see your face in her flanks.

Once again Missy had hired Dodge Rayburn and his truck and trailer to get Merry Jo to the fairgrounds where the show was being held. Missy had reserved a stall as soon as she knew she was going to ride. And she had also reserved a box in the grandstand right next to the ring. It held six chairs and had her name on it. And this was where we were going to watch Missy ride.

It was still daylight when we got to the fair-grounds with Merry Jo. Dad and Missy rode in the truck with Dodge Rayburn, and Mom and I rode in her VW.

The evening show started at seven o'clock, and by that time the lights were shining under the oak trees that made a grove of the fairgrounds. There were lots of people and horses around. Row after row of stalls stretched down under the trees. Some of the tack rooms next to them displayed ribbons won earlier on this first day of the show. There was bustle and an air of excitement all around and I liked it. Even though I kept reminding myself that someday I would be a part of it (perhaps next year), still I liked it.

Mom and Dodge and I went straight to Missy's box, but Dad stayed with Missy to saddle Merry Jo and remain right with her up to the minute Missy entered the ring.

There was one class before the Jack Benny. It ended and nothing happened for a few minutes. Then suddenly the loudspeaker announced Class 29, the Jack Benny. This was it. At one end of the huge ring was a stage with a pipe organ on it. Following the announcement, the pipe organ began to play, the gate at the opposite end of the ring was flung open, and the horses began to enter. It was not a large class this year. Only six horses.

"Here comes Merry Jo!" I cried, so loud that Mom said, "Shush." But I didn't care.

Missy was wearing a number on her back, number 188. Merry Jo came surging into that ring like the grand champion she was. It had been years since she had seen a show ring, for the Joneses had retired her long ago. But she hadn't forgotten a thing she had ever learned or felt about being a show horse. She was lifting her feet as high as she possibly could, and her beautiful little head was tucked in tight and her little ears pricked gamely forward.

Dad slid into a seat beside Mom. "Just look at that. The old lady and the old champion. It's enough to make you want to weep. Oh, I hope she wins it."

"Even if she doesn't, Cal, Missy will feel it's all been worthwhile." Mom's eyes were glued to Merry Jo as she came around the ring to our side. "Just look at that smile."

They were coming along the rail on our side and were almost at our box when the announcer called for a walk. So Missy walked by us. We could have touched her. Dad said, "You're lookin' good." Which is about the nicest thing you can say to a rider. Then the announcer called for a canter, and away went Missy on the proper lead.

"I couldn't handle that mare better myself," Dad said to Dodge.

He nodded. "She's doin' all right."

I looked at Dad. There was pure joy on his face. He was so proud of Missy he could hardly stand it. I could just tell. After all, it was he who had taught her to ride like that. And he who had given her confidence in her ability to ride English, even at her age. Even to enter a show.

For a second or two I felt almost jealous of Missy. It was she who had put that look on his face, not me. I had seen a hint of it that day I first cantered. But nothing like the pride with which he watched Missy competing in the Jack Benny. For another second or two I wished it were me instead of Missy on Merry Jo. I wanted a chance to make Dad look like that. Then I smiled to myself. It was only a matter of time before I would. From that moment I was determined to become the best horsewoman for my age anywhere around. I felt I couldn't wait until tomorrow when I would saddle up Ethan and take him into our ring. I actually *wanted* to ride.

The announcer called for the riders to line up in the middle of the ring.

"The moment of truth," said Dad with a kind of sigh.

The judge went down the row of horses, asking each one to back three steps and then come forward three. Now and then he made a little note on his clipboard. The suspense was pure agony. And all the while, little Merry Jo stood there stretched so that her back feet were almost tippytoe and her nose tucked under. She never so much as switched her tail.

Then the judge handed a slip of paper from the clipboard to the ring steward, who trotted with it across the ring to where the announcer sat.

There wasn't a sound from the audience.

Then it came.

"First place in Class 29, the Jack Benny, goes to number 188, Oakhill's . . ."

You couldn't hear the rest of the announcement for the noise that broke out. A lot of the Morgan people remembered Merry Jo from the days of her prime. And a lot of people had realized that Merry Jo's rider was a very old lady indeed. You could tell it was a popular decision. The applause grew into what is called an ovation.

Missy trotted Merry Jo down to the organ end of the ring and waited there until the other prizes had been awarded and the other riders had left the ring. Then to the sound of the booming organ playing a kind of victory tune, Missy took her victory ride diagonally across the ring, the blue ribbon fluttering from Merry Jo's bridle, and the small trophy firmly gripped in Missy's hand. She was posting faultlessly.

We four raced out of the box and away from the grandstand to where Missy had ridden out of the ring. She was waiting for us and there was a crowd around Merry Jo.

"I did it," Missy cried, and the group around her burst into applause.

"That you did," said Dad and went up and hugged her right there in the saddle and she leaned down to hug him back. Mom and I came up and congratulated her, and then with us walking beside her, she rode down to Merry Jo's stall.

10

Vacation

Dad's and Mom's vacation came on July fifteenth. They each had three weeks, and they decided to spend it here at home.

"After all," said Mom, "we're living in one of the most celebrated vacation spots in the whole world. Where could we go that would be more beautiful than the Monterey Peninsula, and where could we stay that would be more comfortable than this old house?"

"And where could we eat where the cooking would be so good?" asked Dad, grinning at her.

"Flattery will get you anything," said Mom, grinning back.

I always like it when they kid each other.

"Another thing," continued Mom, "it will be a treat for me to have a nice unbroken length of time to pull this place together. There are a lot of things I haven't had time to do since we moved in. And the last thing you need, Cal, is a long automobile trip. The money we save we can put toward another bathroom next year."

"That's a great idea, Lynn. I'm all for it."

As I've said before, I sometimes think my mother has more sense than anyone else in our family. The money spent on a trip somewhere would all be gone in a few weeks. But spent on a bathroom, it would be there for years and years. Of course, trips can be fun, but an extra bathroom is more important, I think. I made up my mind that next year when we started to build it, I would add my savings to it, too. That three dollars a week was adding up. I might use some of it for birthdays and Christmas, but most of it I would save toward the new bathroom.

"Where will the new bathroom be?" I asked, feeling pretty sure I knew.

"Right where your Dad's and my clothes closet is. There's plenty of room there for a shower and toilet and hand basin. And there's plenty of space in the room itself for wardrobe closets." She came across the kitchen and took my face in her two hands. "And the old bathroom will be fixed up nice and pretty for our daughter."

I grabbed her wrists and pulled her hands down and slid my arms around her waist. I was glad I had come to that decision about my savings. But I didn't say anything about it then. I wanted it to be a surprise.

Around the end of July, Missy sprang her own surprise on us. Without a word of warning, she went out and bought herself a truck and horse trailer. The first we knew about it was when she and Dodge Rayburn came rolling up our driveway with the new rig, Missy grinning from ear to ear.

We three were out in the backyard, and as they pulled in, Dad said, "What the—"

Mom burst out laughing. "Missy, you need a guardian. What on earth have you been up to?"

"I've been buying a new trailer and a second-hand truck, and Dodge has been helping me."

The truck was a big, good-looking Chevy-Cheyenne with a camper top, and the trailer was the two-horse kind and looked really sharp.

"I'm really sorry they don't match," apologized

Missy, "but that won't interfere with the way they work. Do you mind if I park them here at your barn, Cal? We'll both be using them, of course."

Dad walked over to the truck and then circled around the trailer.

"Missy, do you really know what you're doing? You've got a lot of money tied up in this rig. How will you ever get your value out of it?"

"I'll be glad to tell you," began Missy. "I haven't had a horse for quite four months, and already I've had to call on Dodge twice. And you never know when you may have to take your horse to the vet's. Dodge isn't always available. Just knowing I have a trailer and a truck to pull it gives me peace of mind. Besides, I can sell them anytime I want to and get most of my money back. And besides that, I'm not going to live forever, though I intend to try. I have worked very hard for what I have, and if I want a truck and trailer I'm jolly well going to have it!"

She had spoken very forcefully, and Dad threw up his hands in mock defense.

"Okay, okay," he said. "I just would hate to have your brother hear about all this and have you declared incompetent."

"He's long considered me that," declared Missy,

"but fortunately he doesn't try to do anything about it. I'm joking. Peter is a very good brother. He mother-hens me a bit too much, but otherwise you can't fault him. Where should we park the trailer?"

Dad and Dodge looked around and decided on a place the other side of the barn. Dodge backed the trailer to where he wanted it. Then he unhitched it from the truck. Now the Ross place really looked like a horse farm. With one horse in the paddock and another in the ring and a truck and trailer alongside the barn, there was no mistaking us. We looked like horse people. I could see that Dad was pleased, although he went on teasing Missy.

"Now that you have recovered from that shock, I have another for you," said Missy when we were all gathered together in the middle of the yard again.

"Nothing you do will surprise me now, Missy," said Dad.

"I've bought Merry Jo."

"You *have?*" exclaimed Mom. "Congratulations, Missy! I'm glad. After seeing you and Merry Jo in the Jack Benny, I hated to think you'd ever be parted from that little mare."

"And that's exactly the way I thought, Lynn. So a week ago I called up Mrs. Jones, asked her what she would take for her, mailed her a check for the amount she wanted, and now Merry Jo is mine."

"That calls for a celebration," said Dad.

So we all went into the house. Mom got out some cheese and crackers. Dad got some cold drinks out of the refrigerator. This July day had been hot, and the drinks went down just fine. Then Dad drove Missy and Dodge back to the red barn in the truck, for Missy had left her car there.

I haven't mentioned Diana in connection with this vacation time because she wasn't around. The day after school closed, the whole Morton family, including Dwight, had gone to Europe for six weeks.

So after the three weeks were up and Dad and Mom had to go back to work, the question was, what to do about me? I couldn't stay alone and I couldn't stay at Diana's. Of course there were other kids on our road that I knew, but I didn't know them well enough to ask to stay at their houses.

The problem was solved when Dodge Rayburn told us that one of the young ladies who helped him exercise his horses was planning to organize a day camp for a limited number of kids. Mom put my name in right away. The camp would go for two weeks. That left just one week before Diana and her family came home. Missy said she would be responsible for that.

The day camp turned out to be fun. There were four kids altogether, all girls. Mom would drop me off at the red barn with my bag lunch and Dad would pick me up there when he came home.

As you might imagine, horses were the theme of this day camp. There was a time I would have hated the whole idea of it, but now I found it was fun. To begin with, I knew more about horses than the other three girls, who were having their first experiences with them. And now I knew how to ride, which they didn't. For another thing, I really liked the young lady who was conducting the day camp. Her name was Jane, and she was a real neat person. She was very pretty, with blond hair and brown eyes. And she was a big girl, the way I was going to be.

Then there was Sam. The first morning my Mom dropped me off at the end of the long, straight, potholed driveway and I opened the gate and went into the yard, I saw Sam tied to the bar outside the barn. Dodge and Jane came out of the barn as I walked up.

"Isn't that Sam?" I asked.

"Yep," said Dodge, "that's Sam."

"He's one of the horses we're going to use for the day camp," Jane explained.

"Could I be the one to ride him?"

"Sure," she said. "What made you choose him?"

"Because I've already ridden him once."

I told her about the morning so long ago when my father had brought me here to look for a horse.

"Well, Sam's your horse for the next two weeks," she said.

The other three girls arrived while I was saddling Sam. And while Jane was explaining everything to them, I rode Sam across the big yard to the ring, opened the gate from atop his back, and took him inside. It was fun to walk him around and remember how scared I had been that first day. As I'd ridden Ethan so much, who is lively and spirited, Sam did seem very tame, just as Dad said he would be. But still I liked him and was glad he was going to be my horse during the time of the day camp.

Even though I didn't go away from home for the whole two and a half months of my summer vacation, I don't think I could have had more variety in it. There was the fun of staying home in our new horse farm with both my parents and doing things with them. Then there was the day camp. And finally, there was the week with Missy.

She came to our house every morning around eight-thirty when my Mom was getting ready to leave. We would go out to the barn and groom and tack up the horses. Then we would go out on the trail or ride in the ring. We liked best to go out on the trail.

In the afternoons we played Scrabble and talked. It was August now, the month of my birthday. I was eleven and would be going to Middle School when school started next month. I got some nice things for my birthday. Mostly school clothes from Dad and Mom, and a shoulder bag from my grandmother. But Missy gave me the best present of all. She gave me a dictionary. It was not a little kid's dictionary but a real college dictionary, the kind real students use. It's been a great help in the writing of this book. And it was a great help when I played Scrabble with Missy.

The day she brought the game out to our house, she said, "This is a fine game for anyone who is going to be a writer."

But after playing with her for a while, I began to

doubt what she had said. I beat Missy almost all the time. And she is a writer. The trouble with Missy is that she tries to find a hard word to fit the spaces. Well, I don't know many hard words, so while she is trying to come up with one, I see where one of my plain ones will fit.

She's awfully funny when I beat her. She calls me a conscienceless brat with no respect for her old age. And we laugh and laugh.

One day we got to talking about Martin. I don't remember how it came about. Probably I said something about how my dad wouldn't miss him so much now that I could ride out on the trail with Dad and could talk with him a lot about horses.

"Melinda, I think you worry too much about how your father misses Martin. It's been almost six years now since Martin died. The world belongs to the living, dear. Your parents will never get over the pain of losing him and they'll never stop loving the memory of him. But I can't believe they are continually grieving over him. What makes you so sure they are?"

"Because they never talk about him. Never."

Missy thought a moment. "I'm sure they did when he was first gone, only you were too little to

162

remember. I think probably the reason they stopped mentioning him was because of you. I think they began to realize that you were feeling guilt because you were the one who was left. And so to help you overcome this feeling, they stopped talking about the one who was lost."

I just sat looking at her across the Scrabble board. I couldn't think of anything to say.

"Let me tell you something that happened on the trail one day when your dad and I were out riding," she went on. "I deliberately brought up the subject of Martin. I knew how you felt about him and the loss of him and I thought maybe I could say something that would help both you and your dad. But I didn't need to say anything at all."

"What do you mean?" I asked. My heart was beating quite fast.

"Your father told me all about his son, his long illness and tragic death. 'It must have been a terrible time for all of you,' I said. He answered, 'Yes, it was certainly that. But I was a lot luckier than many men who lose their sons. I had a most wonderful little daughter. I had Melinda.'"

Missy's face became a wavy blur as my eyes filled with tears. "Did he really say that?" I whispered.

Missy rose and came around to where I sat and gathered me onto her little lap and I put my face down on her shoulder and cried. She just patted me and let me cry, and when the storm was over she began to tell me all the ways she thought I was special. She found a lot to say and I didn't believe half of it. But it was good to hear. Very good.

I thought as I went for the box of tissues Mom keeps on the kitchen counter that maybe, if I worked at it, I could get used to the idea that I had made it up to Dad for Martin.

II

Mostly Missy

Middle School was lots harder than Valley Hills. I was in the sixth grade now and had more homework. So I didn't have as much time to spend on this book. But I worked on it whenever I could.

As autumn moved into winter there was less time for riding. The days kept getting shorter, so Dad and I spent more and more time in the ring. We only went out on the trail during the weekends. It just got dark too soon.

Dad was riding Merry Jo most of the time, since Missy rode less and less. I began to be a little worried about Missy. I could understand her not riding so much. As winter came on and the days got colder, it wasn't so much fun. But there had been little rain. Hardly a day when you couldn't ride. The drought had become really serious. There still was no water in the Carmel River and the trails were dusty. Imagine, dusty trails in December!

On one of the last times Missy had been up to ride, she and I were in the ring together. We had been cantering side by side when suddenly Missy pulled Merry Jo to a full stop. Ethan and I shot past her before I could stop him. When I turned him to look back, I saw Missy take a tiny bottle from her jacket pocket, shake a small pill out of it, and pop the pill into her mouth. She sat her horse for a full minute after taking the pill, then she rode to the gate, opened it, and rode off toward the barn. I put Ethan into a canter and caught up with her.

"Is anything wrong, Missy?"

"Nothing serious, dear," she told me. "Don't say anything about it."

Of course, I didn't. But I began to worry a lot.

It was about the middle of December when Missy got the idea she would like to breed Merry Jo.

"But you know she's barren," Dad reminded her.

"I know they all say she's barren, but they also say she is perfectly normal in every way, no scar

166

tissue in her womb, perfect ovulation, regular heats. Everything normal. But as you said once, Cal, she isn't normal or else she would become pregnant. I want to find out what's wrong."

"What do you have in mind to do?"

"I want you to trailer her over to Dr. Vance's hospital and leave her there for a while and see if he can find out what's wrong."

"Okay," said Dad. "When do we start?"

"As soon as I've made arrangements with Dr. Vance."

A few days later, not long before Christmas, Missy, Dad, and I were in the truck and Merry Jo in the trailer on our way to Dr. Vance's large animal hospital over on the Salinas highway. There we unloaded the mare, and one of the hospital helpers put her in a paddock with a shed at one end.

"This may take a few days," Dr. Vance told us. "How long were you planning to leave her?"

"As long as necessary," Missy answered.

So we said good-bye to Merry Jo and started home in the truck, leaving the trailer behind.

"Why this sudden desire to breed Merry Jo, Missy?" Dad asked as we were leaving the hospital grounds.

"I have suddenly realized that I'm not going to be

able to ride forever," replied Missy, "but I still want to be involved with horses. Having a little foal coming along every year to train and play with would be the answer."

"Missy, you're going to be riding for the next ten years," Dad said, "and Merry Jo will be carrying you."

"I'm not so sure about that," said Missy.

I was listening to this conversation with mixed emotions. It was wonderful to think we might have a little foal like that one at Morgan Manor at our barn someday. On the other hand, I had not liked the tone of Missy's voice when she answered Dad about her next ten years of riding. There was a note in it that made me think she knew something we didn't know, and the worry I had been feeling grew in me.

A few days later, however, some exciting news from Dr. Vance drove everything else out of my mind for the time being. Missy phoned to say he had found there was an obstruction somewhere in Merry Jo's reproductive organs (I can't remember all the technical terms) that prevented a stallion's semen from reaching the egg produced during each of her cycles. He said a minor operation would correct it and Missy had told him to go ahead.

"We'll have to wait through her next cycle," Missy explained to Dad, "and then we can breed her."

This was wonderful news. Missy also informed Dad that she had decided to leave Merry Jo there at the hospital so the vet could examine her and know exactly when, during her following cycle, she would be ready to breed.

This added to my worries, because with Merry Jo staying for what would amount to a month at the hospital, I would be feeding only one horse every morning instead of two. Did this mean I would have to give up my extra three dollars a week?

When I asked Missy about this, she said, "I suppose you wouldn't want to take money when you hadn't earned it." She thought a minute. "I tell you what. How would you like to take care of Fancy for me when I go to San Diego for Christmas? I would have to put her in the kennel in any case, and while I wouldn't trust her with everybody, I would with you. She could stay shut in the barn during the day when all of you were gone. I wouldn't want her running loose when you weren't home. I'll pay for her food, but taking care of her would be well worth three dollars a week."

I've always liked Fancy and by now we knew each

other real well. It seemed a good arrangement for everyone, and so I took over the care of Fancy while Missy was away. I loved having her. Missy brought her basket bed up to our place and we put it in my bedroom. I hated to give her up when Missy came home after New Year's.

As I look back on it now, I think there was a special reason for Missy letting me take care of Fancy. Because the other times when she had gone away, she had always put the little whippet in a kennel.

Before Missy left for her brother's in San Diego, she drove up to say good-bye to us, and she had a present for me.

She asked Dad to carry it in for her since it was pretty heavy. While he went out to the car, she and Mom and I went into the living room where there was a fire on the hearth and a lighted Christmas tree in a corner near the fireplace. The room looked very pretty and cozy. I sat down on the floor before the fire while Missy stood in front of the tree admiring everything. We have tree ornaments that we've had since Martin was a baby.

Then Dad came in with the present. At first I thought it was a suitcase. Only it was the wrong shape. Much too square.

"Where do you want me to set this?" Dad asked.

"Right in front of Melinda," Missy answered him.

He put it down and I placed it flat on the floor. There was a big red bow on the handle. I looked over at Missy, not sure what she expected of me.

"Go ahead," she said. "Open it."

I pressed the clasp and the lid sprang up. A typewriter! A portable typewriter! I was so surprised I couldn't say a word.

"I want to explain about this," Missy began. "This is an old portable. It's the one I typed my first book on. But I have had it all gone over and put in first-class shape. As nearly as I can tell, it works as well as it did when it was brand-new."

Dad and Mom began talking at once about how lovely it was for her to give me this, but still I couldn't say anything. To think she had given me her typewriter! And I knew what the gift meant. Missy was sure in her own mind I was going to be a writer.

"You can buy a new electric portable with the royalties from your first book, Melinda," she now told me, exactly as if she had read my mind.

I got up and went over and gave her a big hug and a kiss.

"Thank you, Missy. Now I'll just have to become a writer."

171

"I'm not sure you aren't one already," she said.

"And I'll teach you how to use it," Mom said.

Mom's an expert typist.

My Christmas present to Missy was a written contract to clean her tack for two months. She said there wasn't anything she would rather have and I believed her, for Missy hates to clean tack.

About the middle of February Dr. Vance phoned Missy to tell her it was the right time to breed Merry Jo.

Missy and Dad had already discussed bloodlines and the various Morgan stallions in our part of California that would be best to breed to. Missy had joined several Morgan clubs and she showed us pamphlets that she had received from these organizations as well as some from the breeding farms. Morgan Manor was one of these and I got quite excited at the idea of their fine stallion Waseeka Peter Piper siring Merry Jo's foal. After all, he was the sire of their Mantic Peter Frost, the foal I liked so much.

Finally to my immense pleasure, Missy did decide on Waseeka Peter Piper because not only was he a grand champion, but he was a small horse, as a proper Morgan should be.

"I like the real, typey Morgans," said Missy. "Not these long-legged things they are breeding now and calling Morgans. They look like saddlebreds. I want a foal to grow up and look like Merry Jo. Or Waseeka Peter Piper."

So one Saturday morning Dad and Missy and I trailered Merry Jo to Morgan Manor. Dr. Vance had phoned on Thursday, but there was no way Dad could get the mare up there before Saturday. Dr. Vance said Saturday would probably be okay, but we shouldn't wait longer than that.

Mom wasn't interested in going. But I was. I wanted to see Peter Frost again.

We had picked up Merry Jo at the hospital and were headed north on 101. Mrs. Towers had been told by phone that we were on our way.

It was around ten o'clock when we got to Morgan Manor. Mrs. Towers was waiting for us and gave us a big smile as we drove in. The same dogs circled around us, barking and wagging their tails.

We unloaded Merry Jo and a stable man came and led her into the barn.

"Could I see Peter Frost?" I asked.

Mrs. Towers laughed. "You really like that colt, don't you? He's over this way."

He had grown a lot since Woodside. He didn't look cute any more, but he was still a very handsome fellow.

"Now let's go see Pete," Mrs. Towers said.

I knew she was referring to Waseeka Peter Piper.

He was in a large paddock behind the barn. Beyond the paddock the hills rose sharply. They were brown and bare of trees.

Peter Piper was on the far side of the paddock, but the minute we drew near the fence, he started toward us. He came prancing and shaking his head, making his heavy mane fly about.

Next to Ethan—that day we had first seen him in the mountain meadow—Waseeka Peter Piper was the most beautiful piece of horseflesh I had ever seen. He was much smaller than Ethan, hardly as big as Merry Jo. But he was almost her color, a dark, rich velvety brown. Only under Pete's brown there shone a kind of bronzy light. I don't know how to describe it. He almost glowed. He came whuffing up to the fence and shoved his nose at Mrs. Towers. She rubbed him roughly between the eyes and he pressed hard against her hand, loving every minute of her attention. Then she made a gesture, and he whirled and went tearing off, kicking his heels at the sky and putting on a show.

174

"He's a real ham," Mrs. Towers informed us. "There's nothing he likes better than an audience. He'll cavort like that as long as we stand here. But it's that quality in him that makes him great in a show ring. And he hands it on to his offspring."

"There's nothing I want now but for Merry Jo to be in foal to him," said Missy, her eyes admiringly fixed on the galloping stallion. "Between them they should produce something mighty nice."

"That they should," said Mrs. Towers heartily. "There isn't a nicer mare in the country than your Merry Jo."

Dad said, "Amen," to that as we started back toward the barn. Mrs. Towers invited us into the house, but we had to get back. Saturday is always a busy day for the Ross family.

Merry Jo was to stay at Morgan Manor until it was definitely known one way or the other whether she had been bred. Dad decided to leave the trailer there.

It was around noon when we got back to our place where Missy had left her car. Mom came out on the back porch as we drove in.

"Stay and have grilled cheese sandwiches with us, Missy," she called as we were getting out of the truck.

Missy hesitated, then shook her head. "Thanks, Lynn. I'll take a rain check if I may. Right now I think I've had enough excitement for one day. I'd better get on home and take my nap."

A troubled look came over Mom's face. "Why not have lunch with us and take your nap here?"

For a long moment Missy just stood there as if she were trying to make up her mind. Not a bit like herself. Dad stepped over to her and put his arm around her shoulders.

"Is something wrong, Missy? Would you like me to drive you home?"

She shook her head. "Thank you, Cal. But I'm fine. Sometimes a little heart thing comes over me. It caught me as I was getting down from the truck." She smiled at him. "It's nothing serious. Really."

"Okay, if you say so," he said. "But you mustn't start off if you aren't feeling right."

She nodded. "I wouldn't; really I wouldn't. But I'm fine."

So we saw her into her car and waved her off, never dreaming it was one of the very last times we ever would.

176

12

End and Beginning

Missy is dead. She had been dead a week.

One morning three weeks ago, the phone rang at seven o'clock. Mom was in the kitchen getting our breakfast. Dad had left for his job an hour and a half ago. I was upstairs dressing.

I heard her say, "*Oh, no!*"

Right away I thought something had happened to Dad and I went tearing downstairs.

"What is it?" I asked.

She held up her hand to silence me, but I wouldn't be silenced.

"Tell me. Is it Dad?"

She shook her head. Then I heard her say, "Is

there anything we can do, Mr. Zinn?" And I knew it was Missy. So my worries had not been for nothing.

She hung up the phone and turned to me.

"Missy has had a severe coronary. She is in the Intensive Care Unit of the Community Hospital. A neighbor took her there early this morning."

"Is she going to die?"

"Nobody knows at this point. But she is in very serious condition. Mr. and Mrs. Zinn chartered a plane and flew up here. They're staying at Missy's house."

"I don't want any breakfast."

"A little fruit juice, maybe?" asked Mom.

"Okay. A little fruit juice."

She went to the refrigerator, took out the pitcher, and poured me a glass.

"You know, dear, people, even old people, recover from coronaries."

I nodded and put the empty glass on the counter. Then I went upstairs to finish dressing for school. My mother's words had not helped the way I felt. In my bones I knew Missy was going to die. Still, I wanted to do all I could to keep her alive, and the most I could do was pray. So I stood there in the middle of my bedroom and prayed that Missy would be allowed to live. But all the time I was remembering that God didn't always see things my way.

Mom talked to me on the way to school. (She takes me to the school now because it's on her way to the office. I take the school bus home.) She tried to reassure me some more, but it didn't help much. I had this awful feeling of dread, and yet I didn't feel like crying. More than anything, I felt numb. Just plain numb.

I don't know how I got through that day at school. I told Diana about Missy, and she seemed sorry all right. But she didn't feel about Missy the way I felt.

So many things would be changed if Missy died. What would happen to Merry Jo? And the little foal that was growing inside her? We had learned only a week ago that Merry Jo was in foal. We had been hopeful that she was when she missed her cycle. Then a month after that, the vet examined her and found she was definitely pregnant. Missy had been so thrilled.

"I just want to live long enough to see that foal," she had said, and everyone within hearing had laughed. Except me.

Now it began to look as if she wouldn't live that

long. The foal would be born next January and this was April. It takes eleven months for a mare to grow a foal. What would happen to Merry Jo? Probably she would be sold back to Pacheco Morgans. And I had so looked forward to having that little foal at our barn!

That evening when we called Mr. Zinn, he said that Missy was no worse but that she was "a very sick girl."

So it went for a week. Every evening we would get a report from Mr. Zinn, and it was never very encouraging. Gradually, though, as days passed, we got used to thinking of Missy at the hospital and more and more hopeful that she would get well.

One afternoon after Dad and I had come home, I stood in my room thinking of Missy and how I should start my homework when my eye fell on the stack of notebooks on my writing table. Suddenly a thought hit me. Would Missy enjoy seeing what I had written about her? It would be the best way I could tell her how much knowing her had meant to me. To all of us.

I went right downstairs and put in a phone call to the Community Hospital. I asked how Miss Zinn was and a very pleasant voice said she "was holding her own." That didn't sound particularly good to me.

"I don't suppose she is allowed to have visitors," I said.

"Oh, no," the voice came back quickly. "She's still in Intensive Care."

"Can she read?"

"Yes, she reads quite a lot. Reads and sleeps."

"Thank you very much." I hung up and went out to the ring where Dad was exercising Merry Jo. She had to be exercised carefully every day now and she was out in the ring all day. A brood mare must not be confined to a stall. Though Dad always brought her in at night.

I waited until he came up to the gate.

"Dad, will you do something for me?"

"Anything within reason."

"Will you take me to the hospital?"

"You won't be able to see Missy, honey."

"I know that. I want to take her something."

He looked at me for a long moment, then he swung off Merry Jo. "I'll unsaddle and be right with you."

I ran off to the house. In the kitchen I got a big

shopping bag and hurried upstairs. Carefully I put all the notebooks into the bag. Each one was numbered, and each one was a chapter long. I had got as far as finishing the Golden West chapter.

Dad brought Merry Jo back from the barn where he had unsaddled her and wiped her down. He put her into the ring, then came to where I was waiting for him in the car.

"Care to tell me what you have in that bag for Missy?"

"It's my book. I thought she might enjoy reading it at this particular time because there's a lot in it about her and Merry Jo."

"I'll bet there isn't anything she'd enjoy more right now."

Two days later we got a phone call just as we were sitting down to dinner. Mom took it, and it was Mr. Zinn saying that Missy very much wanted to see me that evening. We hurried through dinner and Dad drove the three of us to the hospital. Mr. Zinn and his wife were waiting for us in the big central lounge.

"She's not supposed to see anyone but my wife and me," he told us, "and the doctor isn't very happy about Melinda's visiting her. But she insisted so strenuously that he decided it would fret her worse not to see her than the visit would tire her." He turned toward me. "So you are allowed to go in for ten minutes. That's all."

I nodded, and Mr. Zinn led me off to her room. Outside her door he left me, and I went in alone.

"Hi, dear," said Missy, and held her hand out to me.

I went over to her and she took my hand and drew me down to her and kissed me. I kissed her back.

She looked awful. Most of her suntan was gone, she had no makeup on, of course, and her eyes looked sunken and dull. She looked old and very, very frail. I knew as I drew up a chair and sat down beside her that she was going to die. I also knew that I was not going to cry and let her know that I knew.

She motioned toward the notebooks carefully stacked on the bedside stand. "Your book is really good, Melinda. I mean, it's publishable. Of course, I just love it." She smiled at me. "I wish I were as nice as you make me out to be, but I'm glad that's the way you feel about me." She paused as if for breath, and I didn't say a word. "I want you to know, Melinda, that this year with you and your parents and the horses has been the happiest year I have ever lived. I want you to know that."

"I'm glad," I whispered.

She reached toward the bedstand and picked up a card lying there.

"This is the name of my editor and the address of my publishers. When you have finished your book, I want you to send it to this editor and tell her that I told you to send it. She will know what to do with it. Will you do that?"

I nodded. I didn't dare try to speak.

She looked at me quietly for almost a minute while I just sat there looking back at her.

"You're such a dear little girl," she said.

It was time to go. I rose, pushed the chair back into place, and bent over her.

"I love you very much, Missy."

We kissed and said good-night. I never saw her again.

Missy's body was cremated and her ashes put into the sea below her house. This is the way she had wanted it. There was a memorial service for her, and the place was crowded. I've talked as if she had no friends but the Ross family. But Missy had loads of friends all over the country. Her editor flew out from New York. Mr. Zinn introduced us to her, but I didn't say anything about my book. I thought I'd better say nothing until it was finished.

A couple of days after her death, Mr. Zinn phoned one evening to ask if we could all meet the next afternoon at four o'clock at Missy's lawyer's office. Mom's boss let her quit work an hour early to attend the meeting. We couldn't imagine what it could be about.

The lawyer's office is in Monterey at the top of a tall building there. The elevator lets you off right in the waiting room. Mr. and Mrs. Zinn were already there when we arrived. Mr. Wagner, the lawyer, took us down a hall to his office.

He sat down at his desk and picked up a sheaf of papers on it.

"I have here the last will and testament of Muriel Zinn. I have read all of it to Mr. and Mrs. Zinn, but there is a codicil added to it that concerns you three." He looked at Dad and Mom and me. We didn't say anything. Mr. Wagner cleared his throat and continued. "The codicil is dated December 1, 1976. It reads as follows: 'To my good friend Calvin Ross, I bequeath my Chevrolet truck and Miley two-horse trailer; to my good friend Lynn Ross, I bequeath my autumn haze mink jacket; to my good friend Melinda Ross, I bequeath my Morgan mare, Oakhill's Merry Jo, and my white whippet, Fancy.' "

He looked up at us, but we were all three beyond words. For a long time no one spoke, Then Dad turned to Mr. Zinn and said, "Does this meet with your approval?"

"My wholehearted approval," he returned. "But even if it didn't I wouldn't think of going against my sister's wishes."

"I just wish there were some way we could thank her," my mother said.

"She got her thanks in advance," said Mrs. Zinn. "She never stopped talking about the fun she was having with you three and the horses." Suddenly she laughed. "That is, after she decided to let us know she had a horse."

We all laughed then.

So Merry Jo would stay at our barn, after all. And I would have a little foal like Mantic Peter Frost. I wondered what I would name it. And Fancy would be mine. I would own the two living things that had belonged to Missy. But most precious of all would be the living memory of her she had left to me.

A few days later it was Diana's birthday. She is several months older than I am but we are in the same grade. She called to tell me that Dwight's present to her was a promise to take her and any friend of hers to the movie of her choice. She said she had decided to ask me.

That very next Saturday night, Dwight and Diana drove up to my house to pick me up. (Dwight is sixteen now and is allowed to drive.)

Dwight came to the front door, and when I went out, Diana was in the back seat of her mother's two-door. I was going to sit beside Dwight! He handed me in and shut the door exactly as if I had been his date.

When we went into the movie, Diana went into the row of seats first, I came next, and Dwight sat next to me. I could hardly breathe I was so excited. Once he leaned over to whisper something and his shoulder brushed mine! I thought of how here I was on a Saturday night sitting next to Dwight Morton at a movie just as I had imagined I might that day Dad and I drove up to the Granite Ranch.

I sat there staring at the screen, but I wasn't seeing anything. I wasn't hearing anything that went on up there, either. I was busy thinking. I was thinking about this past year, and all that had happened in it. I knew I had grown a lot, not only on the outside, but on the inside, too. And life had got more interesting since I had learned not to be afraid of horses. I knew also that my father was proud of the way I was developing as a rider. I could think of Martin now with sadness for a lost brother instead of feeling guilty about a kind of ghost. I thought of how happy Dad was to have a truck and trailer which he couldn't have afforded to buy. And of how elegant my mother looked in her mink jacket, which she couldn't have had either except for Missy. I thought of dear Missy and of all the fun she had had with us and we with her. And I thought of the little foal I would have next year. Suddenly my heart was so full that my eyes brimmed over. As usual when I am super-happy. I reached down to my coat pocket for a tissue. I tried secretly to dab at my eyes, but Dwight had noticed. I guess he thought I was grieving for Missy. It was only a short time since her memorial service. When I lowered my hand to my lap, he reached over and gave it a quick squeeze. I couldn't believe it!

I turned quickly toward him with a big smile so he would know I wasn't sad. But he was looking straight ahead at the screen with no expression on his face.

Oh, how I wished I were sixteen! But then I quickly realized if I were sixteen, Dwight would be twenty-one. An older man.

I haven't finished this book yet. I want to include in it the birth of Merry Jo's foal. I'm not sure I'll send it to Missy's publisher. Maybe I'll just hold it until I am much older and can make it better. When I do send it off, if I ever do, I'm going to dedicate it to Aranaway Ethan. If it hadn't been for him, there wouldn't have been any book at all.

Doris Gates was born in California and grew up not far from Carmel, where she now lives. An avid horse-woman, she owns three Morgans and spends a lot of time riding the trails through the hills above the Carmel Valley. Two of her horses are featured in *A Morgan for Melinda*.

Miss Gates's many well-known books include *Little Vic*, the Newbery Honor Book *Blue Willow*, and a six-volume series called *The Greek Myths*.